A Poisoned Package

A Murder at the Morrisey Mystery

Book Three

Eryn Scott

KRISTOPHERSON
PRESS
Publishing

Copyright © 2024 by Eryn Scott

Published by Kristopherson Press

All rights reserved.

www.erynscott.com

erynwrites@gmail.com

Facebook: @erynscottauthor

Sign up for my newsletter to hear about new releases and sales!

No part of this book may be reproduced in any form or by any electronic or mechanical means, including information storage and retrieval systems, without written permission from the author, except for the use of brief quotations in a book review.

Cover design by Chris M - Torn Edge Design

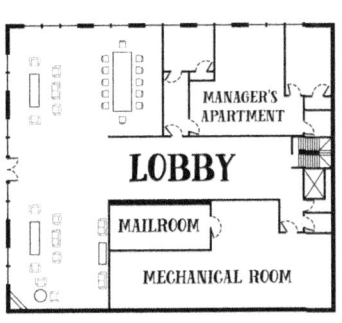

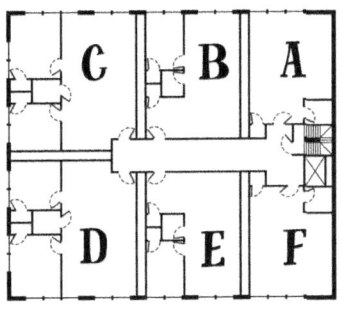
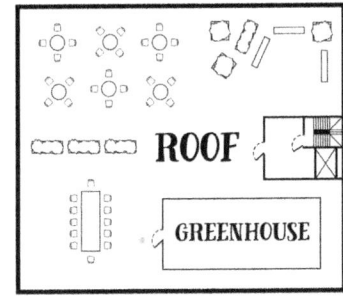

LIST OF APARTMENTS AND RESIDENTS

ROOF	
5C - ALYSSA VERLICE	5F - BAILEY LUNA
5B - IRIS FINLEY	5E - ZOE DAVIS
5A - MEG DAWSON	5D - EDNA FELDNER
4C - W. UNDERWOOD	4F - PAUL KELLY
4B - LAURENCE TURNER	4E - WINNIE WISTERIA
4A - RONNY ARBURY	4D - GREG, OLLIE, LEIA PORTER
3C - KATE, OWEN, FINN, BRYCE O'BRIEN	3F - FATIMA AND URBANE JUNT
	3E - ANDREW SASIN
3B - OPAL HALIFAX	3D - SHIRLEY AND BETHANY ROSENBLOOM
3A - JULIAN CREED	
2C - DANICA AND DUSTIN MCNAIRY	2F - HAYDEN AND TEAL NUTTERS
	2E - ARTURO CORTEZ
2B - DARIUS ROWLAND	2D - VALARIE, VICTORIA, NOEL, MIA YOUNG
2A - CASCADE GRYFFON	
LOBBY	
BUILDING MANAGER - NANCY LEWANDOWSKI	

One

November in Seattle is drizzly at the best of times and downright soggy at the worst.

But it wasn't the rain that had me so disgruntled on that Saturday afternoon—it was the temperature. The Pacific Northwest was having a cold snap, one that hovered just above freezing so we didn't even get the benefit of snow to go with the chilly temperatures and almost-constant precipitation.

"Thankfully, I live in an old, minimally maintained building from the turn of the century. The *previous* one," I grumbled.

"Well, aren't you full of sass and sarcasm today," Ripley said. My ghostly best friend folded her arms and eyed my outfit. "Are you going to a building meeting or on an expedition to the Arctic Circle?"

I tugged at the tops of my wool socks before slipping a jacket over my chunky sweater. "People without bodies do not get to comment on the temperature." I jabbed a finger toward her, knowing if I got too close, that finger would pass right through her spirit. Even though Ripley looked as real as anyone else, to me, I was the only one who could see or hear her.

"Plus," I added, "the lobby's colder than anywhere else in the building. I'm not taking any chances." I zipped my jacket all the way to my chin.

She snorted out a laugh as I reached for my gloves. "Maybe you wouldn't be so cold all the time if you'd chosen a job that didn't include you sitting in one spot all day, poking a paintbrush at a canvas."

I narrowed my eyes at Ripley. "You really want to question my career right now?"

Her hands were up in a flash, regret twisting her mouth into an apology. "No, no. You're right. I just got you back on the right track with your art. I will not jeopardize that, no matter how much I want to poke fun of you for being a wimp about the cold." She stifled a laugh.

Rolling my eyes, I walked over to the couch where my black kitten—now more of a lanky teenager—was curled in the heated bed I'd bought her.

"You're the only one here who understands me," I whispered to Anise before planting a kiss on her fuzzy head.

My down jacket made a rude sound as I stood up straight —like a sleeping bag, only decidedly worse. I didn't meet Ripley's amused gaze as I left for the meeting downstairs.

It was possible that Ripley was right about my sedentary job, though, because after walking down four flights of stairs, I was quite warm in all my layers. The folding chairs set up in the Morrisey's lobby for the meeting were already filling up, and it looked like things were just about to get started. I slid onto a chair at the end of a row, next to Wendell Underwood.

The lobby was crowded, making it seem like every one of the building's residents was in attendance, at first glance. I knew better, missing certain residents too much to forget their absence. Laurence was still in Japan on work, much to my continued displeasure. My friend Zoe was also gone, having left that morning for a weeklong trip to her newfound family's mountain cabin for the Thanksgiving holiday.

I slipped out of my jacket, because now that I was surrounded by the rest of the residents, it was officially too hot. Shooting Ripley a warning look not to comment, I motioned to another open seat in the very middle of the row ahead, showing her I could just as easily sit up there. She swallowed, knowing I'd chosen the end of a row so she wouldn't have to worry about one of my neighbors accidentally sticking an elbow through her spirit.

Luckily, something else seemed to catch Ripley's attention, something she wanted to make fun of even more than me—which was saying something. I followed her gaze, full of amusement, to where Nancy stood behind her podium at the front of the room. The manager of the Morrisey apartment building was frowning down at a laptop, poking at keys with a stiff index finger like the thing might bite her if she left her hands close to the keyboard for too long.

"Oh, I can't wait to hear what this is about," Ripley practically purred as Nancy turned the laptop so the screen faced the rows of us sitting in front of her.

"It's blank," Paul called from the row in front of me.

"I don't have good internet here at work, so it'll have to

stay that way." The voice that met Paul's comment wasn't that of Nancy, but it rang out from the speakers of the laptop. Based on the dramatic, elongated flair, it was our fourth-floor neighbor, Winnie Wisteria.

"We could've filled you in, Winnie," Wendell called from my left, hurt coating the statement as if he wondered why she hadn't trusted him to accurately report the meeting minutes.

Nancy cleared her throat. "I asked Winnie to call in, actually. She's one of the residents who I want to speak about a problem we've been having lately."

Whispers wandered through the collection of residents. What could it be? The secret passages connecting our apartments had been boarded up by a contractor last month.

"I know we cannot see you, Winnie, but can you see us?" Nancy checked.

"Yes, I can see all of you. Proceed." Winnie's tone was clipped.

I got the distinct feeling that we were all about to be scolded. A quick glance over at Ripley, and her subsequent shrug told me she wasn't aware of what was going on either.

Okay, maybe I do need to get out a little more, I conceded.

In fact, based on the nervous energy building between my neighbors, I might be the only one who wasn't sure what was going on.

"Morrisey, there's only one item on my agenda today." Nancy's voice rang out, quieting the residents who'd been having side conversations while she set up the tech. "It appears that our increased vigilance with who we're letting inside the building hasn't done enough. Packages are being stolen from people's doorsteps, right and left."

Knowing the residents of our building as well as she did, Nancy paused to let those who'd had something taken whisper about it to the people next to them. From the row in front of me, Julian complained about an expensive pair of earbuds that had been swiped. Bailey talked about an order of vitamins the company said they delivered but she'd never received.

"They took the socks I ordered." Darius said way louder than anyone else. His cheeks reddened as the group looked his way.

"And I had an expensive piece of art stolen, one I'd saved for months to buy," the voice from the computer called out. "It was taken from right outside my apartment last week."

"Art?" Darius asked. At first, I thought he'd mistakenly thought Winnie was talking about his best friend, Arturo, but then he added, "That's a pretty big thing to steal. What did it look like?"

"It's a painting of a cow lounging on a sofa. It's titled *Cowch*. Get it?" She paused. When no one said anything, she added, "It's one of a kind. Quite expensive."

"She has to be joking. Is she joking?" Ripley asked through a wild laugh.

I didn't dare join in on Ripley's laughter. We couldn't see Winnie, but I was very aware that she could see us. Even letting a smile peek through seemed dangerous.

Nancy's mouth was set in a grim line. "As you can see, the problem has grown too large for us to ignore. I know no one will like this, me least of all, but I think we need to return to having all our packages delivered to the mailroom where they can be locked away safely until you can pick them up."

Groans erupted around me. No wonder Nancy had asked Winnie to call in for the meeting. She needed all the backup she could get when it came to convincing them this was a necessary step.

"But it was so fun opening my door to packages," Darius said dejectedly.

Art patted his friend's back in sympathy as his own shoulders sagged forward. "Like Christmas every time."

"So now we have to wait until you can get them for us?" Cascade whined from the back.

Nancy swallowed, bobbing her head. "I'm afraid so. I don't want to spend my time rushing back and forth to unlock the mailroom, either, but with everything that's happened over the past six months, I doubt you want me to give each one of you a key." She fixed the group with a sidelong glance that asked someone to challenge her.

Murmurs of dissent died quickly. Despite my overly warm state, I shivered. As much as I wanted to believe I could trust every one of my fellow Morrisey residents, the events of the past summer had taught me differently.

"Are we sure it's not an inside job?" Ronny Arbury, grocery deli manager by day and improv actor by night, cut an overly obvious glare at a blonde teenager near the back of the room. "Someone *new*?" he emphasized.

Like embarrassed parents whose child said something rude to a stranger, the residents of the Morrisey widened their eyes in warning at Ronny. The nineteen-year-old may have been present at the meeting, but the earbuds in her ears showed she wasn't listening.

Despite everyone's warning looks, Ronny pointed to his

ears and then flashed a questioning glance at Julian as if to ask, *Are those your missing earbuds?*

Taylor Feldner, the great-granddaughter of Edna Feldner, had moved into 5D last month. And while the teen wasn't listening, she didn't miss everyone turning to look in her direction.

Taking out her earbud, she raised her dark brows. The question was clear, even though indifference coated her expression. Why were we all looking at her?

"Your great-grandmother isn't missing any packages, is she, Taylor?" Nancy asked.

Taylor shook her head and stuck her earbud back in place.

Nancy sighed as the group turned their attention back to her. "I know it's not ideal, and not much of a Thanksgiving gift to everyone, but I've already talked with the mailman, and I'll put signs up for the other delivery companies. We'll start Monday. Okay, that's it. Meeting adjourned. Off you go." Nancy swatted at them and swiveled her laptop back toward her.

"Well, that was fun for a minute, but definitely not what I expected," Ripley scoffed.

Wendell turned to me and said, "Any plans for Thanksgiving, Nutmeg?"

The man's wild eyebrows were the only hair on his head. His face was clean shaven, as was his scalp. The Art Deco lights in the lobby of the Morrisey shone off its shiny surface.

"I'm going to be here at the Morrisey dinner," I told him. "You?"

"Ah, I'll be with my reptile group. We're getting the

snakes together for a little social time." He smiled, revealing straight white teeth. Was it just me, or were his eye teeth a little sharper than a normal person's?

"Oh." I swallowed. "I didn't know snakes needed ... social time."

His shoulders bounced in response. "Well, even if they don't, we certainly do." A hissing laugh spilled out of him, something I felt sure he'd practiced to sound more reptilian.

I busied myself by helping stack the chairs in our row. Just as I was grabbing my coat from under the chair, my phone buzzed in my pocket. I fished it out and grinned.

"Oh, I know who that is based on your smile," Ripley said in a mocking tone. She winked seductively as she added, "I'll see you up in the apartment. Have fun texting with Laurie."

Even her teasing couldn't erase my good mood as I turned my attention back to my phone. A text from Laurie greeted me.

> Hey, any way I can ask a big favor? I think my new card got delivered to my apartment instead of coming here. Can you go check my mail pile so I don't worry it's floating around in the mail or in the hands of some criminal?

I'd heard all about his lost debit card last week, and how he'd found the old one after canceling it and ordering the new one. My heart went out to the guy for yet another inconvenience in the saga.

Wetting my lips, mostly as a way to wipe the smile off my lips, I responded:

A Poisoned Package

> Sure. We're just finishing up a building meeting. I'll check right now.

It was getting late his time, so he must really need the peace of mind that the card had arrived. I wondered if he would need me to send it to him if it had been delivered here. I threaded my way through my neighbors toward the stairwell.

Taking the steps two at a time, I stopped briefly on the second floor to check his texted response.

> What was the topic today? Did Nancy threaten to evict anyone who'd try to deep-fry a turkey?

I sputtered out a laugh. I hadn't been here last Thanksgiving, but Aunt Penny had told me all about Hayden Nutters almost burning down the whole building by trying that little stunt on the roof.

> Nothing that fun. We have to start picking up packages in the mailroom. Too many are going missing.

Sending my response, I kept jogging up the stairs, stopping at the fourth floor instead of going up to the fifth. Fumbling with my key ring, I located Laurie's key as I headed to apartment 4B.

Across the hall, something caught my eye. Sitting on the doormat outside Winnie Wisteria's apartment was a package. It was about the size of a book, maybe a little bigger. A hardback? Or it could've been something much more valuable. If she was at work, as she'd mentioned on the video call, she might not get home until later this evening. None of us knew what she did for a living; the woman was secretive most of the time, dramatic always. But given that the package placement in the mailroom didn't start until Monday, I wondered if I should grab the package for her for safekeeping until she came home.

All thoughts of mail were punted straight out of my brain as three excited barks came from apartment 4B. From behind the door, a hushed, deep voice said, "Shhh, Leo. You're going to ruin the surprise."

"Laurie?" I called, trying to shove the key into the lock even though my fingers had forgotten how to work.

The door swung open. Laurie stood on the other side, holding on to the collar of his brown-and-white pit bull, Leo. The dog's tongue lolled out of his mouth as he strained forward, trying to reach me. As much as I wanted to wrap my arms around Laurie, my nerves got the better of me. So, as I stepped inside, closing the door behind me, I sank to my knees and held my arms out to receive the excited dog first. Laurie let him go, taking my stance as a green light. The next few seconds were a blur of tail wagging, panting, and licking, as Leo wiggled in front of me.

"I see how it is." Laurie cocked an eyebrow. "I come all the way from Japan for you and you hug this guy first?"

Pressing my lips together, I stood. "You came all the way ... for me?" I swallowed as I finally looked up into his dark brown eyes.

"I mean, my boss thinks my mom really needed me home for the holiday, which she definitely told me she did, but ...

yeah." His lips tugged into a handsome smile. "I missed you, Dawson."

Channeling all my bravery, I inhaled and lunged toward him, wrapping my arms around him so tight that he let out a quiet "Oof."

"I missed you too, Turner." Without being too obvious, I breathed in his spicy, soapy, Laurie smell. "But you're just back for the holiday?" I asked, eyeing his suitcase sitting next to the kitchen as I stepped back.

He dipped his chin. "Unfortunately, yeah. I found out that I'm going to be there until the new year, at least. The good news is that I was able to extend my trip to ten days instead of the five they wanted, which is great since it feels like I've been traveling for two days straight." He snorted out a laugh.

Happiness surged inside me. Leo returned after leaving to grab a toy to show me, tail wagging. The large dog leaned his body against my leg.

"So, what do you say to having dinner with me?" Laurie reached back and rubbed his neck.

Beaming, I said, "Of course ... but, you know that it's, like, only two o'clock in the afternoon, right?"

"It is?" Laurie groaned and ran a hand down his face. "I'm sorry, I have no idea what time zone I'm in at this point."

I patted his arm and glanced out the window. "It's okay. With how gloomy and rainy it is out there, it feels like it's the evening. Plus, I didn't have lunch, so I'd love to do an early dinner."

Laurie's face broke into a grateful smile, but it dropped as he looked around. "I don't have any food here. We'll have to go out."

"That's okay. I'll just need to stop by my place real quick to grab my wallet."

Shaking his head, Laurie said, "My treat, Dawson."

My lips quirked. "Okay. If you say so." Patting my jacket, I said, "Then I'm all set."

Laurie and I apologized profusely to Leo, as we had to leave him behind, but once he was safe in his cozy crate, we headed out the apartment door. I stopped short, eyes fixed on the other side of the hallway. Laurie ran into me, not having expected me to freeze immediately after stepping over the threshold.

"Everything okay?" His hands settled on my shoulders as he peered over me.

Grimacing, I said, "I don't think it is." I strode forward and pressed the buzzer next to Winnie's door. Nothing. Turning back to Laurie, I pointed at the doormat. "Winnie's not home, and there was a package here a few minutes ago. I think someone stole it while we were inside your apartment."

Now I really wished I'd grabbed that package for Winnie.

Two

I shoved Laurie back inside his apartment before he could shut the door. Leo cocked his head in question from where he sat in his crate, wondering why we hadn't left. Laurie gave me a very similar look.

"I told you that was what our meeting was about just now." I jabbed my finger down toward the lobby of the building and then shut Laurie's door behind us. "Whoever's been stealing the packages just took that one when we were right across the hall." Guilt overwhelmed me. "We've gotta tell Nancy."

But Laurie didn't move. He raked his knuckles across his jawline as he seemed to get an idea. "What if we did a little more investigating before we went to Nance?" His brown eyes danced with excitement. When I frowned, he added, "Come on, Meg. I had to sit in Japan while you went through that case this summer. Let me help you with this one."

I couldn't say no to Laurie under normal circumstances, but especially not when he looked at me with that dimpled smile and a glimmer of playfulness in his eyes. "Fine." I let my shoulders slump forward in defeat. "What do you have in mind?"

"I came in through the back entrance, so you're the only one who knows I'm home." He paced in front of me. "What if we set up a fake package on my doorstep and wait and see for ourselves who's taking them? If Nance is starting the mailroom change Monday, you guys might never find out who it is."

Swallowing, I contemplated his idea. I exhaled any reservations. "It's worth a try."

He smiled, teeth raking over his lip as he tried to keep his grin contained. "I have just the thing." Laurie moved to the kitchen counter, where I'd been placing his mail. He grabbed a package I'd brought in for him last month. "This is printer ink. Easy to replace if I end up losing it." He held it forward like an offering. "Now, as for catching the person if they do come by ... I wonder if I can rig a camera under the door without it being detected on the other side."

I scratched my neck. I didn't mention that I had a ghost at my disposal whom I could ask to sit out in the hall and watch for us. Nobody—not even Laurie—knew about my ability to speak to ghosts.

"Or we could just take turns watching through the peephole."

His head jutted back. "And give ourselves eye cramps? I don't work in the tech space for nothing, Meg." He leaned closer and whispered, "Just give me this, okay?"

I agreed with a chuckle as he moved to his desk, opening a drawer and rummaging around in it until he found a small camera. It looked about as big as the one in my laptop, but it wasn't attached to anything so it must've had Bluetooth capabilities. He carried it over to the door, stopping by the kitchen to grab some duct tape.

"Anything I can help with?" I craned my neck to see what he was doing as he knelt by the door and held the camera in the small opening between the bottom of the door and the floor.

"Since we're not going out, do you want to have food delivered? There's cash in my wallet on the counter," he called over his shoulder.

I couldn't help but smile. He was having too much fun.

Pulling out my phone, I decided on a Peruvian restaurant. They didn't deliver, but it was right across the street and Laurie loved the place. I could brave the rain for a few minutes.

By the time I had the order in, Laurie had the camera paired with his laptop and was taping it onto the bottom of the door.

"Remember, I'm going to need to get out to grab the food." I frowned as I listened to how much tape was going into this project.

His eyebrows rose. He hadn't thought of that. Checking out the peephole, he made sure there wasn't anyone in the hallway before opening the door carefully. The camera stayed in place, just barely skimming across the wood floors. Laurie wore a self-satisfied smirk as I grabbed the cash and slipped through the opening.

"I'll be right back."

The restaurant would need more time to make the food, so I popped upstairs to my apartment first. Ripley was waiting for me, staring at the rain dripping down the window.

"Hey, what took you so long?" she asked.

"Long story. Laurie surprised me by coming back for Thanksgiving." I walked into the bathroom and ran deodorant under my arms before checking my hair. It was in a messy bun, one I hoped looked more artistic and effortless than disastrous.

Ripley appeared in the bathroom doorway, eyes shining. "Oh, and are the two of you going to have a romantic dinner out?" She squinted one eye. "At two thirty in the afternoon?"

"It's an early dinner. His internal clock is all off." I sniffed my breath and then chugged a shot of mouthwash, swishing it around my cheeks. I spat out the mouthwash, rinsing out my mouth after that. "And, it's going to be more of a romantic dinner in, actually. We're doing a sting operation to see if we can catch the package thief."

Ripley deflated slightly. "Meg." My name was a warning. "Ninja Turtles. Need I say more?"

"You absolutely need to say more." I wrinkled my nose. "That was super vague."

"Don't get friend-zoned again." She crossed her arms. "You said it yourself that it's hard to go from having a shared love of the Ninja Turtles when you were kids to trying to start something romantic. Well, you've finally got him looking at you like you want him to; don't fall back into friend-zone stuff."

I drove out a frustrated sigh. "But we *are* friends. That's what makes us so great. He's a friend that I want to kiss. I don't want to lose the friendship stuff just because I want to add the kissing stuff."

She chewed on her lip. "I know. It's just ... it's a fine line. I don't want you to get hurt again."

"I won't," I assured her. "It's Laurie. He came home for me." I tapped my finger on the bathroom counter. "Well, and his mom, but he said it was mostly for me." I blew her a kiss before heading toward the door.

Ripley got out of my way so I wouldn't breeze right through her. "Need any help? With the mail-thief sting operation, not the date, of course."

A chuckle escaped me. "Laurie's got this whole spy camera setup going on down there, so ... definitely."

She broke into a grin. "I'll stay in the hall, I promise." She held up three fingers even though I knew she'd never been remotely outdoorsy like a Girl Scout was required to be.

"Sounds good. I'm going to pick up our food and I'll be back."

The jog across the street to grab our order had me rain soaked and miserable by the time I made it back to the Morrisey. But the delicious aromas wafting up from the bags of food clutched in my cold fingers made it all worth it.

I'd barely stepped out of the stairwell when Laurie's door opened and he ushered me inside. It was dark in the apartment, only the dim gray light spilling in through his tall windows offered any help seeing where I was going.

"I'm guessing the camera's working," I whispered, stepping over the sacrificial package he'd already placed in front of his door.

He nodded. "It's a good thing I don't have a doormat like Winnie, or the height would've blocked the camera, and we wouldn't have been able to see anything. Removing it at this stage might've given us away. As it is, we'll have a full view of whoever comes out of the elevator or from the stairs."

He showed me over to the command center he'd created at his kitchen bar, helping me out of my dripping jacket and up onto a stool. The laptop sat in between us, the live feed from under the door streaming silently on the screen.

"I've kept all the lights off just in case," he whispered as he slid two plates from the cabinet. The clatter they made caused Laurie to freeze midway.

"Plates are too loud," I said, shaking my head in a swift arc. "We can just eat out of the containers."

Laurie put the plates back as quietly as he could and grabbed forks, clinking his against mine as he slid onto the stool next to me. A small whine came from the crate behind us.

"I'm leaving Leo in there for obvious reasons." Laurie fixed his dog with an apologetic look. "After a few months living with my buddy, he's not listening as well as I'd like, and I don't want him to bark and ruin our cover."

I gave the dog a sympathetic glance as well before digging into my meal.

"So, did your new debit card come to the right address or is it really here?" I whispered in between bites.

"It came to Japan like it was supposed to. I just needed an

excuse to surprise you." Laurie ran his shoulder into mine playfully.

Ripley's advice about the friend zone swam in my mind, setting up worries like precariously stacked packages. But I had no idea how to make eating less of a friend activity, so I continued to watch the feed with Laurie as we chatted about everything that had happened since we'd last talked.

Just when I thought we weren't ever going to see a thing, the door to the stairwell eased open. It was the softness of the motion that caught my attention. I had to do a double take to make sure it was even moving. That wasn't the routine shove of a resident on their way to their apartment. It was wary.

The hairs on the back of my neck stood on end as I peered closer at the laptop screen. Laurie, noting my interest, leaned forward too.

I held my breath, not wanting to jump to any conclusions just yet. I'd had many a moment where my arms were full and a slow opening of the stairwell door was necessary so I wouldn't jostle the contents in my arms or disturb the tenuous balance with quick movements.

The breath I'd been holding released in a long whoosh as the person walked forward into the line of the camera. It was Julian Creed, our neighbor from the third floor. I sat back.

But Laurie reached out and wrapped his hand around my knee, a gentle warning.

Frowning, I watched as Julian scanned the hallway and then tiptoed forward toward the package at Laurie's door. Quick as a cat, Julian plucked the package off the ground.

The slide of the cardboard against the floor just ten feet to our right made me want to shudder. But I suppressed that response. I didn't want Julian to hear.

Laurie glanced back at Leo, giving him a nonverbal warning to stay silent. The dog's ears were forward, and he watched the apartment door, but he didn't bark.

And just like that, Julian was through the stairwell door, slipping back just as quietly as he'd come.

Ripley wandered through the wall, eyes wide with confusion as she came in from the hall. In true Ripley fashion, she said, "Oh, it's all dark and sexy in here."

"But ... but Julian had something stolen as well," I muttered, ignoring my friend's comment.

Ripley and Laurie gave me the same look, one that clearly marked me as too trusting.

"Of course, he would lie about that." Laurie's tone was gentle, as if we were still trying to remain quiet. "What better way to take suspicion off him?"

Chewing on my lip, I had to admit that he was right. "*Julian*. Julian?" The first was a scolding, the second a question. "But he's a finance bro. He's got all those fancy suits and boring stories about portfolios and trading."

"Rich people steal sometimes too," Ripley said, jerking her shoulders in a shrug. "Maybe he likes the thrill."

"I wouldn't call him *rich*, but..." I froze as I realized I'd said that out loud in response to Ripley.

Her eyes were wide, and they jumped between Laurie and me. Luckily, my response to Ripley wasn't nonsensical in the context of my conversation with Laurie, and he didn't seem fazed by my non sequitur comment.

"I know," he said, "But we definitely have to tell Nancy about this now." He clicked a few things on the laptop—saving the video footage of the theft onto his desktop—before closing it and giving a clipped nod toward the door.

I peeled myself off the stool and sank onto unsteady legs.

"Julian's a thief?" I repeated in awe, the truth still not sinking in.

"Well, look at it this way, you've suspected him of a crime before," Ripley said, referring to earlier this summer when I'd spent the better part of a day thinking he'd killed his neighbor, Mr. Miller. "Now you don't have to feel badly for thinking ill of him."

I couldn't bring myself to smile.

"Small consolations," Ripley muttered.

Detaching the camera now that we no longer had any need for it, Laurie held the door open for me. I dragged myself into the hallway, Laurie following behind with his laptop. On our way down the stairwell to the lobby, there were no games from our teenage days. This wasn't the time for competitions such as *how many steps can you skip* or *how far can you slide on the railing*. We stood in front of Nancy's door in somber silence.

Laurie pressed her buzzer and the manager's door opened.

Nancy's small reading glasses were perched on her nose as she took us in. She tipped her head up to see Laurie and took in an abrupt gulp of air.

"Laurence, what a fantastic surprise." She swatted at his arm as if she might actually be mad about his unannounced appearance. "Gimme a hug, you." She wafted her hands toward herself.

Smiling, Laurie obliged, letting Nancy squeeze him far too tightly before she let go.

"Are you back for the holiday?" she asked, assuming this to be a social visit. "Oh, your mother is going to be so excited to see you." Her mischievous gaze flitted over to me for a split second, showing that she knew I was included in the list of people happy he was home.

"I am." Laurie's tone sank at the end of the statement. He winced as he added, "Unfortunately, we're here to talk to you about something a little less pleasant." He patted the laptop tucked under his right arm.

Nancy's gaze skittered through the quiet lobby hallway. Voices drifted down from the fireplace room by the front doors, proving the Conversationalists were in their normal spot. "Here, come in. Come in." Nancy stepped aside and beckoned us forward.

Ripley followed as Laurie and I entered.

Nancy's apartment always smelled nice; that was what happened when a retired baker lived with a building full of residents who loved to eat. She was constantly whipping up some treat or another. But today, the scents of orange and cinnamon were added to the usual delicious combination of sugar, flour, and butter. The tart smell sat in the air like the spritz from a peel suspended in time.

"What are you baking?" I asked before I could remind myself not to get distracted.

Nancy clasped her hands together. A small bit of flour poofed off her fingers in the process. "Cranberry orange muffins. Just tweaking my recipe for Thursday." Her smile faded as she looked from me to Laurie, remembering why we were there. "Okay, what's going on?"

"We found out who's been stealing packages." Laurie walked over to the counter and set his laptop down, opening the lid as he explained our fake package sting operation.

I wasn't sure if Laurie was concerned that Nancy wouldn't believe him, or if he was just going for a dramatic reveal, but he refrained from telling her who it was until the man came on the screen. Nancy covered her mouth with her hand. Laurie paused the video just after Julian grabbed the package.

Adjusting her reading glasses—even though they hadn't moved a millimeter—Nancy huffed out a breath. "Well, I suppose we should go talk to him."

Laurie closed the laptop and tucked it back under his arm.

"Oh? All together?" I balked. I didn't enjoy conflict. Accusing someone of stealing felt like the ultimate confrontation.

"Of course. I might need the proof you and Laurie collected." Nancy tsked as she shooed us out of her apartment and shook her head. "Though, I'm sure there's a perfectly good explanation for this. Maybe he was trying to keep the package safe for you."

As naïve as that logic sounded to me, I had been about to do the same with the package on Winnie's doorstep before I'd seen Laurie. Maybe I should be more like Nancy and think the best about my neighbors.

Laurie wrapped his free arm around my shoulders, squeezing me to him in encouragement.

Together, the three of us tromped over to the elevator and started the trip up to the third floor. There was a bit too much déjà vu for my liking, this having been the exact floor where we'd found Mr. Miller's body this summer.

Shaking off the memory, I reminded myself that this was completely different. Julian was just ... hoarding the packages from the building for completely normal reasons. There would be no bodies in this situation. Right? Laurie tensed, too, proving he'd noticed the similarities.

If she was nervous, Nancy didn't show it. She knocked on the door with all the force of a woman on a mission. When we didn't hear anything, she knocked again. Then used his buzzer.

"Julian. It's Nancy. We need to talk."

No response came.

After another round of knocking and buzzing, a door opened, but not the one in front of us.

Opal Halifax stuck her head out of her apartment next door. Her chunky red glasses made her already wide eyes look even larger. "What's going on here?"

"Manager business, Opal. You know what it's like." Nancy flapped a hand toward the older woman.

Opal nodded. She *would* know, having been the building manager here for decades before Nancy took over. Understanding or not, that didn't get rid of Opal's curiosity, and she continued to watch from her doorway as Nancy mashed her finger down on Julian's buzzer yet again.

"Too bad I can't go in to check if he's there or not," Ripley said from my side.

Her ghostly rules were clear, and unless she'd set foot in a place during her life, or I crossed over a threshold, she couldn't enter. I'd never been inside Julian's apartment, not even during the summer when I'd found the secret passages. His door had been nailed shut, like most of ours were now.

"Maybe he's not here," I suggested, playing on Ripley's comment even though I'd been the only one to hear it.

Behind us, another door opened. I flinched as the voices of the Rosenbloom sisters spilled out from their apartment. "What's all the fuss, Nanc—Oooh." Bethie and Shirl spotted Laurie. "*Laurence*, we didn't know you were back." They bustled forward.

Fear flashed in Laurie's eyes. I stepped in between them, sacrificing myself. The two older women might look like the co-presidents of a crochet club, but they were deviants when it came to Laurie. I wouldn't put it past them to paw at him or pretend he had a stain on his shirt with the hope he might take it off and they'd get a glimpse of his abs.

I was about to open my mouth, hoping something commanding would come out that might shove the Rosenbloom sisters back into their apartment, when a loud thud came from inside Julian's apartment. The sisters froze in their approach. A gasp escaped from Bethie.

"Julian, I'm coming in," Nancy narrated, fear flashing over her features. She pulled out her key ring, searching for the master key she had in case of wellness checks—like this.

My heart hammered in my chest. My vision zeroed in on

Julian's door as Nancy unlocked it and pushed her way inside.

"So much for hoping he wasn't home." Ripley cringed as she glanced into his apartment.

Because there was Julian, splayed out on the floor, unmoving.

Nancy's voice ripped me out of my stupor. "Someone call nine-one-one."

Three

Opal Halifax was by my side in an instant, bounding forward on those spindly legs of hers. Her phone was in her hand—looking far too bulky in contrast to her lithe, bony fingers, but she said, "I'm already calling. Go help."

Laurie and I raced forward as Opal talked to the dispatcher. Laurie set his computer down before moving next to Nancy. In all the madness, I noticed Ripley wandering through Julian's apartment, but I couldn't pay attention to her in the moment.

I fell to my knees. "What's all of this?" I studied the dozen or so brown squares littered around him. My brain was in such a panic that it didn't recognize what they were at first. "Chocolate?" I asked as things finally snapped into place. A box of chocolates lay next to him, scattered on the floor; the one next to his hand had been bitten in half.

"It looks like he was eating them when he…" Laurie gulped, sounding just as dazed as me.

"They want to know if he's breathing," Opal called from the threshold, her phone still pressed to her ear.

We scanned him, searching for signs of life. He was lying face down, but his back moved up and down.

"Barely," Nancy called. "Tell them to get here quickly. He may have eaten something poisonous." She eyed the candies, toeing away the one nearest to her.

"But we *just* saw him." I squeezed my eyes shut for a moment to try to clear my head.

Being bombarded with too many sensory inputs at once was making me feel dizzy. One worry rose above the rest. The package Julian had stolen last had been Laurie's. What if the box he'd thought contained printer ink, had actually been full of these chocolates?

Eyes flying open, I said, "Where's the box he stole from you, Laurie?"

Laurie perused the space, his attention freezing on the kitchen counter—the same tall kitchen counter we all had in our apartments. Julian's, however, was piled with boxes. Ripley was still inspecting them, though she could only see what was already opened. Packing materials flowed out of the ones he'd looted. Other boxes were still mostly intact as if he'd recently swiped those. Laurie's package was on the counter, unopened. So the chocolates weren't meant for him. My heart rate slowed in response.

"I think I found Darius's socks," Ripley called from over by the couch. "Oh, and here are Bailey's vitamins."

My attention turned to Laurie as he wandered over to the package graveyard, rubbing at the back of his neck. "I guess he couldn't get rid of any of these boxes in the trash or recycling for fear that we might see them."

"Why would Julian be stealing from us?" My question edged on panicky.

Nancy, still monitoring the man's breathing, swung her head sadly. Her reading glasses shifted, and she pushed them back into place.

I whirled on Opal. "You're his neighbor. Have you noticed anything strange about him lately?"

"Other than him stealing everyone's stuff?" The old woman's nostrils flared as she released a quick huff of aggravation. At my scowl, she held up her hands and said, "No, I didn't know about any of this. I don't know the ins and outs of what happens in my neighbors' lives."

Laurie and I exchanged a wry, disbelieving glance. Opal was the epitome of nosiness. Nancy cocked an eyebrow as she pulled her attention away from Julian for a moment. But it was Shirl Rosenbloom in the hallway who muttered, "If that's not the biggest lie I've ever heard…"

Opal blinked, but she didn't even try to fight it. "Fine." She bristled. "I know things about my neighbors who do *interesting* things. Julian was never one of those."

"He was more interesting than you thought," Laurie said as he surveyed the boxes. He frowned, leaning closer over an empty box next to the edge of the counter. "I think this could've been the one that held the chocolates." He read the address label. His expression turned cold. "It was a package for Winnie."

"The one I saw at her door earlier." My stomach sank.

Nancy studied the box of chocolates on the floor. "There's a card under here." She used the toe of her shoe again to scoot the box off it and turned her head so she matched the angle of the card. Her eyes narrowed. "It says, 'Winnie, congrats on another year.' But it doesn't say who it's from."

I peered down at it. A cute sticker of a frog wearing cowboy boots was stuck in the corner of the note card. "It could be from anyone. Another year of *what*?" I mused, but it was cut short by squeaking shoes and barked instructions as the paramedics arrived.

The Rosenblooms were shoved back into the hall with Opal. Nancy, Laurie, and I stepped into Julian's small kitchen as the EMTs turned him over. The rain must've picked up outside because their uniforms were soaked; water flicked off them with each practiced movement. In her haste to move away from the rainwater flying off the team, Nancy pushed me into Laurie. His arm wrapped around me, pulling me close as we watched the paramedics work, and I sank back into him, glad I had his support during this terrible ordeal.

"These are the chocolates he ingested?" one EMT asked, moving the box out of the way while the other inspected Julian's pupils at the same time she checked his pulse.

Nancy confirmed that they were, as far as we knew.

His skin was almost blue. What breathing he was doing was now rattled and erratic.

"Opioid overdose," an EMT said with a certainty I didn't feel. "I'm administering four milligrams of Narcan." The woman moved so quickly I barely had time to register the small device before she stuck it in his nose, depressed the small plunger, and began counting as she held on to Julian's wrist once more.

My heart was in my throat as they waited a predetermined amount of time, shared worried glances as they saw no change in his condition, and delivered a second dose. Laurie's hand tightened on my shoulder as the seconds ticked by, becoming minutes.

Just as I was losing hope, the paramedic exhaled in relief. "He's stabilizing."

Julian blinked his eyes open. One of the paramedics moved behind him, helping him sit up. They began talking to him, letting him know where he was and what happened. He was still very wobbly and dazed as he answered the paramedic's questions about his name and the day of the week.

One EMT moved toward us as she pulled off her gloves. "You saved his life by calling when you did." To her partner, she said, "Let's get him ready to travel."

They were just lifting Julian onto the stretcher when Detective Anthony walked into the apartment. Like the paramedics, she and her team dripped with evidence of the pouring rain.

Her gaze focused on Julian at first, but it quickly moved to me, Nancy, and finally Laurie. Recognition flashed over her stoic features. Memories hit me of her laughing and flirting with Laurie this summer when she'd been here to help with Mr. Miller's murder. As if she were recalling the same scenes, the detective's gaze lingered on Laurie, clocking how I was tucked in front of him, how his hand now wrapped protectively over my shoulder.

If Detective Anthony felt anything, she hid it deep

beneath the surface. "What do we have here?" she asked the paramedics.

The majority of them bustled about, solely focused on getting their patient to the nearest hospital, but one EMT stopped to fill the detective in on how Julian had been suffering from an opioid overdose and they'd administered naloxone. Detective Anthony tipped her head, giving them the okay to leave, and saying she'd be by the hospital later to question Julian. With that, she turned her attention to us.

"We think he might've eaten poisoned chocolates," Nancy said, pointing to the spilled candies on the floor, some of which the EMTs had smashed in their haste to save Julian's life.

Detective Anthony's eyes brushed over the scene, cataloging everything. "What are all of these boxes?"

Cringing, I stepped forward. "We just discovered that Julian may have been stealing packages from the residents in our building. We came to confront him but heard him collapse instead. He was in the middle of eating candy from one of the packages he stole today."

"So, the chocolates, the *poisoned* chocolates, were not meant for him?" Amaya Anthony's mind seemed to be working quickly. Snapping her fingers at one of the members of her team and calling for an evidence bag, she donned a pair of gloves before picking up the note card that had been attached to the chocolate box.

"I think everything's here except Winnie's art," Ripley called as she emerged from a stack of boxes.

As if my ghostly friend had summoned our dramatic neighbor, a shrill voice cut through the hallway. "Is my art in there? Did he take it?" Winnie Wisteria shoved through the throng of Morrisey residents and police, proving word of the stolen packages had spread. She perched at the edge of the police tape, but craned her neck to see inside the apartment.

"Is that Ms. Wisteria?" Detective Anthony held up the card she'd been analyzing, cocking an eyebrow as if to ask if it was the same person.

We all nodded in confirmation.

She swiped two fingers in the air, signaling to her officers stationed by the door. "Please let that woman through. I want to talk with her. The rest of you—I want this place searched for evidence of opioids."

The officers surrounding us fanned out, and Winnie rushed forward, blue satin scarves and a mauve waterfall cardigan wafting behind her.

"Did you find my painting?" She repeated the question, eyes scanning the room.

Detective Anthony brought out her notepad. "I'm more interested in the fact that Mr. Creed almost died eating chocolates that he swiped from your doorstep. Were you expecting such a package?"

Winnie balked. "Poisoned chocolates? Why would I expect that?"

The detective held up the note card so Winnie could read it. "They were addressed to you. This card came with them. Mr. Creed stole them from your doorstep, as he's been doing with many of your neighbors, it seems. Unless I'm mistaken, and my team finds evidence of drugs in the apartment, I'd say someone was trying to kill you, and they got Mr. Creed instead." She fixed Winnie with a scowl.

My neighbor sputtered, "W-why would anyone want to kill me?"

"That's what I'm asking *you* to tell me." The detective handed the evidence bag to a passing officer. "Where were you this afternoon?"

"I was at work." Winnie's gaze moved nervously around the room.

Nodding slowly as if it might elicit more information, the detective asked, "And where is that?"

Winnie glanced at us but lifted her chin. "I work at the Third Avenue Theatre."

Surprise flitted through me. The theatre wasn't unexpected. We'd always assumed Winnie was an actress. She was more dramatic than anyone I'd ever met. The shock I experienced came from her admitting as much. Attention-seeking as she may be in certain ways, when it came to her personal life, the woman was about as open as one of those stubborn pistachio shells that have zero cracks and are impossible to split.

From the lack of surprise in Nancy's features, our building manager already knew about the theatre. We had to provide financial information upon moving in, so her employment status was likely on file. But Laurie's grip tightened on my shoulder, showing me I wasn't alone in finding that tidbit interesting.

Jotting down the theatre name, the detective pressed her mouth into a line. "I'll repeat my question. Is there anyone who might've wanted you to eat those chocolates instead of Julian Creed?" Her tone grew thinner, likely a good indication of her waning patience.

Winnie crossed her arms. "I don't know what you're talking about. Everyone loves me."

The detective pinched the bridge of her nose. "Look, Ms. Wisteria. I have two stabbers on the loose in the city right now. Not one. Two. I can either help you investigate this attempt on your life, or I can go back to helping people who want it."

My chin jutted back. Detective Anthony must've been stressed. While the woman was always no-nonsense and focused, she wasn't normally rude.

Winnie flipped her scarf behind her. "I don't need any help. I'm sure these weren't for me. It's all a misunderstanding."

The detective sighed. "Okay. Officer Garrison, would you bag the chocolates, the box they came in, and that shipping box there on the corner so we can check them for prints?" she asked one of the crime scene techs she'd brought with her. The woman bowed her head a touch, and the detective turned back to us. "You're all free to go ... for now. I know where to find you if I have more questions—if I don't get called back here for another murder in the meantime," she added under her breath.

Unsure of what else to do, Laurie and I wandered into the stairwell. Our feet dragged as we climbed up to the fourth floor, hesitating on the landing. Ripley floated nearby, as if she, too, were dazed, and following me was the only thing she knew how to do.

"Oh, your jacket." Laurie snapped his fingers, gesturing toward his apartment. "It's still at my place."

I followed him into the hallway. He unlocked his door,

letting it swing open so I could grab my coat. I draped it over my arm, swallowing. "I should probably let you get some sleep." My overwhelmed brain couldn't do the math to figure out what time it was in Japan, but I didn't need numbers to know Laurie was exhausted.

"Actually, I was going to take Leo out for a walk. If I can stay up for a little longer, it'll help dull the jet lag." He grimaced at the cold, dark, wet city outside his tall windows. "Want to come with?"

I curled my fingers into my palms, pressing my nails into my skin to keep me grounded in my excitement. "I'd love to."

"That's my girl." Ripley winked in my direction before she disappeared, leaving me and Laurie alone.

Four

The next morning, Laurie and I met to grab coffee before walking up the hill to Harborview Medical Center to visit Julian. Ripley had gone ahead earlier to see what she could find out.

Since the walk up to the hospital was on the steeper side, and according to our neighbors, we had "the youngest legs," we were sent as the building representatives to check on Julian.

To be fair, Laurie and I had already discussed going together during our walk yesterday. But when we passed by a large grouping of residents in the lobby on our way out that Sunday morning, and told them where we were going, they sat back in relief and asked if we wouldn't mind filling them in on his condition.

"I mean, I feel terrible for the guy, but he did take my socks," Darius said as Laurie and I pushed through the building doors and walked out into Pioneer Square.

The air was crisp and held just the mistiest sprinkles of rain, which was highly preferable to yesterday's downpour, especially since we had to walk. We ordered our coffees and chatted about Laurie's long trip from Japan as we waited, continuing the conversation on our trip up the hill.

But when we arrived at the emergency wing, they wouldn't let us see Julian.

"He's not able to have visitors yet," the nurse at the front desk explained, turning us away.

Luckily, I caught sight of Ripley near the edge of the waiting room. Telling Laurie I was going to the restroom, I wandered over in her direction and jerked my head for her to follow me. The restroom was one of those single-person setups with a locking door and the sink inside, so I would be able to talk to Ripley without freaking out anyone else by whispering to myself in a stall.

But the moment I turned around, the grave look on Ripley's face stole away any words I might've said, any questions I might've asked.

At first, I wondered if her bleak expression was due to where we were. Harborview had been where both she and my mom had died after the car accident. They'd been rushed here, but none of the following surgeries or life-saving measures had worked to revive anyone—except me.

My theory about her grave mood being about the past fell flat, however, as Ripley croaked out, "Julian is..." She gave a quick jerk of her head as if she still couldn't believe it. "He's in a coma."

"What?" I asked at full volume, doubly grateful for the

private restroom. Still, there were people just outside the door, and I didn't want them to hear me talking to myself. Whispering this time, I added, "But he was fine yesterday."

Ripley physically deflated. "He was okay for a while, according to the nurses. They're pretty freaked out too. They feel awful."

"What happened?" The need to understand clawed at my throat, at my chest, making it hard to breathe.

"I was still trying to figure out what room they had him in when Detective Anthony showed up this morning," Ripley said. "I listened as they told her she couldn't see Julian Creed because he'd relapsed and had gone into shock. Apparently it's not uncommon for someone to seem like they're okay after that Narcan stuff, especially the two doses it took for them to revive him. The place got busy, and they didn't catch the signs before it was too late. By the time they realized what was happening, they were just able to stabilize him enough to keep him alive, but he hasn't woken up since."

Squeezing my eyes shut, I tried to focus. "I mean, at least he's still alive?"

"That is the upside to the whole situation." Ripley ran a hand through her hair. "Though, they're not sure when or if he'll come to."

Exhaling, I motioned to the waiting room. "I've gotta get back to Laurie. Would you stick around for a while to see if there's any change?"

"Sure, Megs." Ripley gave me a small smile. "I'll let you know if I hear or see anything."

"Thanks." In a daze, I left the restroom.

Laurie's eyes narrowed in worry as I staggered over to him. "What's wrong? Are you feeling okay?"

"It's Julian. He's ... he's in a coma."

"How'd you find that out? I thought they wouldn't tell us anything since we aren't immediate family."

Oh, right. In my stupor, I'd totally forgotten who I'd learned that information from. Inwardly scolding myself, I gestured to the hallway I'd gone down to find the restroom.

"I overheard some nurses talking while I was in the bathroom. And unless there's another guy from the Morrisey who overdosed on laced chocolates yesterday, he's the one they were talking about."

The news settled over Laurie in a wave of what looked like fatigue.

A man bumped into me as he tried to move past us in the crowded emergency room waiting area, and a woman coughed on Laurie. We both immediately began moving for the doors, needing to get out of this space. As we walked back the way we'd come, I explained everything *I* had overheard—so what if it was through Ripley—about Julian's condition taking such an abrupt turn for the worse.

It was a good thing that Laurie was a diligent listener, because upon returning to the Morrisey, I couldn't seem to bring myself to tell our waiting neighbors the awful and shocking truth. Something about seeing their faces light up, expecting positive news from us, made me choke. So, Laurie filled them in.

The group had grown since we'd left for the hospital, and it seemed more like an unofficial building meeting at that point. Our neighbors' reactions ranged from gasps of horror to heads hung in shame, especially Darius, who took back everything he'd said earlier. Socks weren't important when it came to someone's life.

Just as Nancy was wondering if anyone knew how to get ahold of Julian's brother to ask if there was anything we could do to help, Winnie strode into the lobby.

"Winnie, did you hear about Julian?" Art asked.

Barely pausing, Winnie said, "Nope, and I don't care to. That man is dead to me."

"She's closer than she realizes with that prediction," Opal said in a wary singsong tone.

Either Winnie didn't hear her or maintained that she didn't care, because she kept walking.

"Winnie, aren't you worried about the chocolates?" Ronny Arbury called after her.

"Nope," she said, waving a hand in a goodbye as she stepped into the elevator.

"Why won't she admit that she needs help?" I wondered aloud.

"Because she's Winnie, and she's just as stubborn as she is secretive." Nancy's tone was low, almost sad.

"But someone was trying to kill her. Not Julian. Her." Laurie slipped his hands into his pockets as we stood around the group.

A few more Morrisey residents wandered over, and I noticed the Rosenbloom sisters again stood closer to Laurie than was socially acceptable.

"It feels absurd not to do anything when a person tried to

poison Winnie." I looked around. My neighbors nodded in agreement.

"But what can we do if she won't accept help? Force ourselves into her life?" Opal asked, even though I was sure the meddlesome woman had done the same thing more than a few times.

Ronny Arbury lifted a finger. "I overheard her say she works at the Third Avenue yesterday. They're doing a production of *Singing in the Rain* right now. I'd bet anything she's in that."

Laurie's expression softened with an idea. "And if she was working yesterday, on a Saturday, it's probably fair to say she spends a lot of time there. I'd bet anything the threat is connected to her work. Based on the note that was with the chocolates, it sounded like she'd just celebrated an anniversary of some sort. It could be an anniversary with the Third Avenue."

"The theatre world can be pretty cutthroat." Ronny's tone was grave, as if he knew all about it, as if his days were spent on the stage, not pricing roast beef in the deli he managed.

"Ronny, do you think you could get a part in the production and keep an eye on her there?" Laurie asked.

Ronny's cheeks blushed red. "I, uh, I mean, I *would*, but I ... well, I already tried. I auditioned a few weeks ago and they turned me down." He adjusted the neck of his sweater. "They said I'm much more suited to improv."

My guess was that the advice probably sounded a lot more like, *stick to improv, buddy*, but I wasn't going to be the one to question him. As if he'd heard my inner thoughts, Ronny looked at me, causing my cheeks to heat with embarrassment for a moment.

But then he said, "They did have some openings in the props department. Maybe Meg can get a job painting backgrounds and be our inside man."

I considered the idea. My paintings had been selling over the past few months, so I wasn't in dire need of a second job. But selling a painting here and there was less steady than I wanted my income to be, and a side gig didn't seem like a terrible idea. The only hitch was that Laurie was home. I didn't want to miss out on spending time with him.

Correctly interpreting my uncertainty, Laurie leaned close and said, "I still have work to do during the day, so don't worry about being gone for my sake."

I ignored the tingle of pleasure that rushed up my neck at the warm brush of Laurie's breath so close to my ear, and said, "I could do that. I'm not sure if they'll want me, but I can at least interview."

My Morrisey family spent the next few minutes denying that anyone would ever *not* want me and giving me advice about what to wear, look for, and ask about tomorrow when I went. I spent the rest of the day finding my portfolio of work, putting together an updated resume, and even picking an outfit I hoped screamed, *hire me!*

Ripley didn't return from the hospital until later that evening. Her expression was drawn, and all I could get out of her was a sad shake of her head. There hadn't been any improvement to Julian's condition.

Somehow, that knowledge made infiltrating the Third Avenue Theatre even more important. It didn't matter that the person had ended up poisoning the wrong victim. Whoever was behind this was a potential murderer, and I was going to make sure they couldn't hurt anyone else I cared about.

THIRD AVENUE THEATRE

FIRST FLOOR

- STORAGE
- CLOSET
- TICKETS
- PROPS
- LOBBY
- PIT
- STAGE
- WOMEN'S TOILET
- MEN'S TOILET
- CLOSET
- GREEN ROOM

SECOND FLOOR

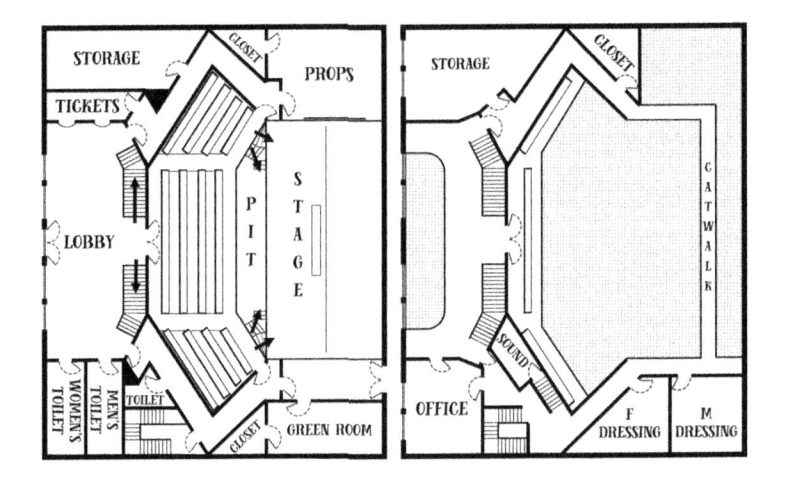

- STORAGE
- CLOSET
- CATWALK
- SOUND
- OFFICE
- F DRESSING
- M DRESSING

Five

Monday morning, Ripley and I split up. She went back to the hospital to keep an eye on Julian, and I went to the Third Avenue Theatre to see about a job.

It only took me minutes to arrive at the ivy-covered brick building since it was just a few blocks up the hill. Other than her love of drama, I could see the appeal behind working here for Winnie.

Unlike the more grandiose Fifth Avenue and Paramount theatres over by the convention center, the Third Avenue was a modest playhouse with just over two hundred seats instead of two thousand. In its online reviews, the way patrons stuck to writing about its historical charms—added to the sheer number of times they brought up supporting small local theatres—had me guessing the productions were nowhere near the quality of the larger theatres to the north.

Laurie and I had looked for a website last night after Leo's walk. And while the theatre technically did have one, it hadn't been updated in four years, so I figured just showing up would be my best bet.

Straightening my spine and taking one last fortifying breath, I checked the front door. It was locked, but a woman stood just inside by the ticket booth. Knocking on the glass, I waved until I caught her attention.

At first she didn't move. Even through the old glass windows, I could see her consider ignoring me before she finally walked over. The lock clicked open and she pulled the door toward her.

"*Whaddaya want?*" she asked in the quickest, most disinterested way I'd ever been greeted—if I could even call it a greeting, considering how clear it was that she did not want to speak to me.

"I'm here to inquire about a job in the props department," I said, patting the portfolio I clutched at my side. "I'm an artist."

The small woman looked me up and down. Her eyeliner was spotty, like it might've been left over from yesterday's makeup, and her short dark hair was messy. She probably couldn't be bothered with it either.

Chuffing in aggravation, she said, "Fine," and stepped aside so I could enter.

The lobby was beautiful. The ornate carpet with its tones of navy blue, teal, hunter green, and purple brought to mind peacock feathers. A tall Christmas tree stood off to my right, reaching up into the cutout in the ceiling that looked down on the lobby from the second story. Directly in front of me were huge doors that must lead to the stage, flanked by twin staircases that led up to the balcony.

I'd expected mildew and dust to be the predominant odors, but the theatre smelled ... cozy, like pine and spice. The smell of dust was present, but it was muted, hanging in the background like the Art Deco chandelier, yet another reminder that the place was probably close to a hundred years old.

"I'll take you to the director," my new *friend* said as she motioned for me to follow.

Stepping forward, she pulled the house doors open, both at the same time, like she might be some small theatre version of Aragorn from *The Two Towers*. All movement ceased on the stage as the actors watched us enter. The few people seated in the audience turned to look as well.

The auditorium was charming, with dark wood bench seating and a large stage with room for an orchestral pit in front. Despite the beauty, a terrible clamminess settled over me, and all feelings of coziness I'd gathered in the lobby of the theatre disappeared. I hated being the center of attention like this, especially when it seemed we'd interrupted a rehearsal.

Gulping, I resisted rushing behind one of the pillars holding up a small balcony, which ran the perimeter of the back three sides of the theatre, and followed after the angry woman instead. But each step down the slightly sloped floor leading closer to the stage made my skin crawl even more.

"Carter, this girl would like to apply for the props department," the woman said, her words far too loud and jarring compared to the smooth voices of the trained actors that had filled the space just before we arrived. She jabbed a thumb back toward me as if the people might not know who she was referring to.

A man with a bald head, white beard, and circular glasses peered around her to study me. Rallying as much bravery as I could, I stepped forward, offering my portfolio instead of my hand.

Carter slid his fingers around the portfolio, slowly taking it as his eyes narrowed on me. Between his blue eyes and the scarf wrapped expertly around his neck, he painted an intimidating picture. He brought the portfolio to his chest but didn't open it.

The woman from the lobby huffed as if she didn't have time for this and turned to escape back to the ticket booth. Honestly? I considered rushing after her.

"Thank you, Francine," he called after her but then turned his attention back to me. "Props, huh?" Carter drawled. It wasn't a Southern accent, but the words slid from his lips in a bored manner that made me feel like he was about to make fun of me. Then he said, "An artist creates an interesting opportunity, actually. We finally have someone to paint those sets you built and were putting off finishing, Damien," Carter added loudly enough for the statement to carry to the stage. Flipping through my portfolio, he said, "I was going to have some of these sets built, but how do you feel about painting big canvases? I've got a bunch of flats in the back for you to work with."

"I can do *flats*," I said, not strictly clear on what those were. Based on the way he'd described them, they must be close to backdrops. I'd never painted anything that big, but how hard could it be?

"Come on, Carter, just tell her she's got the job," a female voice called from the stage.

I looked over to find a striking woman with long, dark hair, who had to be about my age, shading her eyes from the spotlights on stage and tapping her toe.

"Yasmine's right, we can't be picky when we're desperate." An equally stunning blonde woman walked out from behind the side curtain, hand on her hip. Two men occupied the stage as well, but neither was as distinctive as their female counterparts.

Jaw ticking, Carter continued to page through my portfolio. "All the same, Imogen, I'd like to look."

"Shouldn't Petra be doing that?" An aloof male voice came from somewhere behind the curtain, but I couldn't see who it belonged to.

Carter slammed my portfolio shut. "I'm the director. I will make this decision." Spit flew from his lips as he snarled toward the stage. Reworking his face into a calmer version, he looked at me. "You're hired, Miss...?"

"Meg. Miss Meg," I said stupidly. *Miss Meg?* What was I, a preschool teacher? Hating myself, I added, "Meg Dawson."

He pointed to the seat next to him. "Do you have something to write with, Miss Meg?" he asked.

My groan of disapproval at his continued use of the nickname was barely contained as I said, "I have my phone." I held it up as if Carter might need proof that I, in fact, carried a cellphone. "I can take notes on here."

"Nope. We're traditional around here. Paper. Pen!" The words shot out of him, along with a little more spit. "Get the woman a pen and paper."

There was rustling behind the curtain, and before I knew what was happening, a pen came whizzing past my head, clattering about three rows back. A small notepad flapped out from the same shadows but didn't even make it past the first row.

"Really, Damien?" Carter cut a heated glare at the stage. "You could've walked it out to the poor girl." Carter pointed and snapped in one smooth motion at the first row and then behind us.

Interpreting the gesture as an order to me, I grabbed the pen first and then ran up to the first row, shooting an apologetic look at the actors for the delay in their rehearsal. After that, I scuttled back to my seat next to Carter.

Clapping twice, he yelled, "From the top of that scene."

The actors reset and then began the scene over. I wasn't sure what I was supposed to write in the notebook. My last note-taking experience had been back in school. I wrote the date at the top of the notepad.

About five minutes into the scene, Carter tapped his finger on the armrest in between us and said, "We'll need a flat of a house for this scene. Damien's built a city street that we'll use for the red carpet scene you missed before, but it needs to be painted like brick buildings."

I jotted down everything he said, realizing now what the list was for. I hadn't seen *Singing in the Rain* in a while, but it seemed like they were toward the beginning. They ran through the entire play, stopping every few minutes for Carter to call out a command, have them redo a scene with "more feeling," with different blocking, or even once because he'd gotten something in his eye and hadn't seen the end of a dance number.

At one point, he even got so fed up with one of the characters being in the wrong place, he chucked a roll of tape at the man and made him put a big X on the stage to mark his place.

It wasn't just Carter who stopped rehearsal either. Half of the interruptions were fights breaking out between cast members, the most volatile of which were the two lead women, Yasmine and Imogen. Carter did nothing to quell the arguments, however, letting them run their course and then tapping that armrest before telling me to add something else to my list. It wasn't all flats. He had me make a list of things to search for back in the prop room.

It was all, "We've got a couch back there. Make a note to find it." Or, "Velvet ropes for the movie premiere scene. Yes, I think we have those in the back."

One thing was for sure, I was going to find it hard to do any sleuthing if I was so busy creating all these flats and finding all these set pieces. I gaped at the long list I'd accumulated as the actors chatted on the stage after the final scene.

Carter turned to me and said, "Just let Damien know if you need anything else built. He's *fairly* handy with his tools." The disgusted way he said the word *fairly* made me think maybe the elusive Damien was, in fact, not handy at all.

He was the only person I hadn't seen throughout the rehearsal. Well, not the only one. I also didn't see Winnie at all. I wondered if she'd had a small part at the very beginning of the play, something that had happened before I'd arrived. But then Carter turned to face the back of the theatre, and he yelled, "The lights were a mess during that last scene, Winnie. Once we get the musicians in here, you're going to have sound to deal with, too, so use this time to get your lighting cues down. Can I trust that you're going to do your job, or do I have to come back there and do it myself?"

Lights? Sound? I craned my neck back to where a small booth sat in the back corner, perched between the first and second floors.

Winnie peered out of the small booth. "I'll get it, Carter. Don't you worry." Her gaze met mine, and she immediately dropped back down out of sight.

My mouth opened, but what was I going to do, call out to her? Before I could make any decisions, Carter clapped his hands twice just as he had earlier and said, "Okay, Miss Meg. Let's take you on a tour."

Without waiting, he vaulted up the steps to the right of the stage, motioning for me to follow. He wasn't a particularly tall man, but he strode in such an authoritative way that it took me two or three steps to match one of his.

"Standard stuff up here. Backstage, that door slides like a barn and leads into the prop room, and that's the trapdoor." He gestured toward a long rectangle toward the back of the stage.

I was about to ask him if I would be using the trapdoor at all, but he was already turning away. He stopped about halfway across the stage, the bottom of his shoe making a Velcro ripping sound as it peeled reluctantly from something sticky.

Redness flushed across his bald head. "Who used duct tape on the stage instead of gaffer tape?" he roared.

The few crew members who were still hanging around darted away, ducking out of sight. I didn't want to mention that *he'd* been the one to throw the roll of duct tape at Don to mark that spot, making him pull it up once he'd finally gotten down the correct placement.

Before I could blink, Carter raced down the stairs again, and into a hallway that ran along the side of the rows of seats. It was as if our tour was being timed. My lungs burned as I raced to keep up. Meanwhile, Carter pointed and shouted things like "green room," "closet," and "bathroom."

In between, he told me a bit about the theatre. "It was built in the nineteen thirties, and for the last fifty years, only musicals have been performed on this stage."

"Why musicals?" I asked.

Carter whirled on me, wiggling his fingers in my face. "Because musicals make people happy, Miss Meg," he said, sounding not the least bit happy.

Just as quickly as it had paused, the tour resumed. We passed by crew members, their faces a blur as I focused on keeping up—and not running into any walls. Maybe the crew didn't want to mess with the Guinness World Record's fastest theatre tour timing Carter was obviously shooting for because not even one of them stopped to say hello; most of them didn't even make eye contact.

Carter jogged forward and bounded up the staircase to the second floor. I was dragging air into my lungs by the time I reached the landing. Maybe Ripley was right about my severe lack of exercise.

"This is the office. I share it with the owner of the building who operates as a kind of stage manager once we get closer to opening night. If you ever can't find me on the stage, that's where I'll be." Now on the second floor, we traveled back down the hallway toward the stage again. "Dressing rooms for the cast." He motioned to the right, but didn't stop.

We reached the catwalk and I pivoted on my heel, sure we'd be turning around at this point, but Carter surged forward, moving across the small bridge hanging over the stage as if he were some kind of human-mountain-goat hybrid, unaffected by heights. I, a certifiable human-chicken hybrid, clung to the railing and moved as quickly as I dared after the director. Between the lights and the black stage below, dizziness wobbled around my vision. My breath whooshed out of me as I reached the other side.

If I needed a minute to recover, I wasn't going to get it. Carter took off immediately, gesturing toward the different storage spaces along this hallway, a mirror to the other side. He practically slid down the banister of the staircase on the other end. My heel slipped in my haste to follow, and I shuddered to a stop in the lobby right behind him.

"Francine runs the tickets and concessions," he said before disappearing into the first-floor hallway on this side of the theatre.

Movement over by the restrooms on the other side of the lobby caught my eye. A man wearing acid-washed jeans and a camel-colored jacket with its collar popped up wandered through the area, muttering to himself about something I couldn't hear from this far away. He ran his hands through straight hair that seemed to stick up in all directions.

The fact that I could see through him was a welcome

discovery. While the rest of the cast and crew didn't seem to want to talk to me, it was good to know there was at least one ghost here who might be able to help with the information I needed about Winnie and who might've wanted her dead.

But I couldn't stop now to talk to him. Carter was probably halfway to the stage already after my momentary hesitation. I needed to catch up.

Given that it was now the fourth hallway I'd walked down, I was starting to get the hang of things and figured this might be the last one. He stopped in front of a door on the left that was labeled Props.

"And here's your domain." Carter pushed the metal handle down, letting us into the expansive space. "My last prop designer quit. Couldn't take criticism."

Doubt wobbled inside my chest as I wondered if I would be able to, either, especially given Carter's propensity for yelling said criticisms. It had been one of my weak spots in New York City. But before I could voice any reservations, another ghost caught my attention. This one was a woman. She wafted through the different sets and boxes making up the prop room. Her brunette hair was pulled back into a severe bun, and she wore a cream-colored silk blouse with long, loose slacks.

I did a double take as I noticed her transparent state. Her eyes met mine, but even though it was clear I'd seen her, she simply looked away, unfazed, as if she came across people who could see her every day.

Carter opened his hands. "You should find everything you need in here, Miss Meg, but just let Damien or Francine know if you need to order anything."

Tucking the notepad into my back pocket, I told him I would. Quick as my tour had been, I was sure I had questions, but I couldn't think of any at that moment. Mostly, I was tired. Tired and irritable.

Carter must've caught onto my change in mood because he jerked his head toward the lobby and said, "I'll walk you out. You've put in a long day." Sliding his hands into his pockets, he sauntered out of the prop room.

Taking a step back in preparation, like a runner on blocks at the beginning of a race, I jogged after him, expecting the same pace from the tour. I immediately screeched to a halt as I nearly ran into Carter's back. Now that the tour was over, the director practically sauntered. Maybe he really had been going for a speed record up until that point.

At a pace that now seemed decadently slow, we walked back into the lobby. My shoulders settled as we stood in the warm space, the peacock colors calming me down after my marathon day. I hadn't realized how tense I'd been, but now that I was going home, breathing came easily for the first time all day.

"And that's the light booth?" I pointed to the other side of the lobby, not having missed that Carter had excluded that room from his tour.

Carter gaped at me in confusion, as if he wasn't sure why I would need to know anything about that space. "Yes, but you won't need to go up there. It's Winnie's area." He pulled out his phone, distractedly adding, "Petra is the owner, and you'll need to see her about filling out employment paperwork, but she's not in today, so you're free to go."

"Great. Thank you so much." I struggled to think of any

more questions I had for him before I left. "What, uh ... Is there a certain time I should be here tomorrow?"

Carter tore his gaze from his phone long enough to say, "You have just under two weeks until we open to get through that list. Come and go whenever you want. As long as you get it all done."

I saluted the man for some embarrassing reason. "Okay. I can do that," I said, having absolutely no idea if I could.

Without so much as a goodbye, Carter turned his attention back to his phone and stalked through the double doors toward the stage—opening them in the same, two-at-once style Francine had. Maybe it was one of the quirky superstitions about this theatre. I'd have to ask around. But my attention flitted up to the light-and-sound booth.

There was someone else I needed to talk to first.

I scaled the steps to the booth and felt very much like Carter as I rushed into the small room. Winnie, fiddling with a patchboard in front of her, immediately slid behind her desk in an attempt to hide from me.

"Winnie, why are you hiding? I'm here to help you figure out who sent you those chocolates." I couldn't keep the exasperation from my voice, not after one of the longest days I'd had in recent memory.

The woman I'd known most of my life grabbed her purse from under the desk. Rushing past me, she said, "I didn't ask for this. Don't bother, *Miss Meg*." My accidental nickname was like acid in her mouth.

With that, she whirled out of the room, her angry footsteps creaking down the old staircase leading to the theatre lobby.

Six

Puffing out my cheeks, I begrudgingly left the light booth and headed for the lobby as well. I hadn't planned on staying all day, and I was ready to go home.

But as I jogged down the creaky stairs and turned toward the front door, I slammed straight into a hard chest. A quick stagger back and a blink up had me staring at one of the more beautiful men I'd ever laid eyes on. I mean, he had the tall, dark, and handsome bit *down*—to a T. Well, all except his eyes, which were ice blue. Other than that, he had dark, floppy hair that looked as if a woman might've just been running her fingers through it, the perfect amount of stubble for a manly commercial about shaving or knives, and a dark gray sweater that stretched across his substantial chest.

My mouth opened and closed a few times, but before I could say anything, the broody man grunted something and disappeared into the auditorium. There was an anger so palpable emanating off him that I wondered if I'd done something to offend him. I thought through the performance I'd watched today but couldn't remember seeing him in any of the scenes. A man like that, even if he was quiet, had to be a lead actor.

"Don't worry, Miss Meg. Damien doesn't talk to most people. I wouldn't take it personally."

I whirled around to find Francine leaning on the ticket counter, staring. She'd witnessed the whole thing.

That was Damien? *Backstage* Damien? Why in the world were they hiding a gorgeous man like that behind the curtain? He was the one who'd thrown the pen and notebook at me earlier and had taken all sorts of verbal abuse from Carter throughout rehearsal without so much as a single retort.

"I didn't mean to run into him. It was an accident." I closed the space between me and Francine, surprised she was being nice after acting so indifferent earlier.

She wafted a hand toward me. "Oh, he wasn't mad about that. He's just … always angry. You'll get used to it."

Would I? That was the person I was supposed to go to with any prop-building requests. He seemed about as approachable as a full-grown moose.

"Well, thanks. I'll see you tomorrow." I gave her a smile and turned to leave.

"If you last that long," Francine muttered under her breath as I reached the door.

I wasn't sure whether to feel threatened by that, laugh it off, or turn around and confront her. Instead, I pushed through the front doors and walked home. Each step I took away from the theatre seemed to lighten my steps and raise my spirits. My stomach grumbled as I closed in on the Morrisey. I'd skipped lunch, and the coffeehouse I usually went to on the corner of Cherry Street looked crowded. Standing in line and ordering seemed like too much effort.

Opting to settle for whatever I might have in my apartment, I crossed the street and entered the Morrisey. My building was like a hug, especially after the confusing, volatile environment of the theatre. Art, Darius, Opal, and George occupied their normal places in the sitting area to the right when I walked inside. They had a fire going in the hearth, and the scent of pine logs burning mingled pleasantly with the hint of rosemary always present in our building lobby.

"Afternoon, Nutmeg," Darius called, tipping the fedora he wore, in my direction.

The immense gratitude I felt at not hearing the nickname Miss Meg erased any negative opinions I held about my childhood nickname. Nutmeg was *way* better than Miss Meg.

Opal's eyes flashed with interest. "How'd it go at the theatre? Winnie walked in just before you but didn't stop to talk, so we didn't get a chance to ask her."

Not that she would've told you anything if she had *stopped.* I kept the grumpy thoughts to myself.

"I got the job," I said, still not sure if that was a good thing. "I'm sure I'll learn more as I spend more time there."

Glancing right and left, Art asked, "And does it seem like one of them might've sent those death chocolates to Winnie?"

A dry laugh burst out of me. "Oh, definitely. That place

is full of tension, and they all seem to hate each other. I just have to whittle down who could've done it."

George, the only ghostly member of the Conversationalists, smiled reassuringly in my direction. "If anyone can figure it out, it's you, Nutmeg."

I couldn't thank him for the comment since I was the only one who saw him, but I hoped my smile in return showed my gratitude. "Has anyone heard an update on Julian?" I adjusted my bag on my shoulder. I'd be seeing Ripley soon enough but wanted to check whether my neighbors knew anything she might not.

Opal clicked her tongue, and worry sank to the bottom of my stomach.

But then Darius said, "Well, he's still alive."

"Barely," Art scoffed. "They say he's stable, but I'm not sure what's stable about being in a coma."

I inhaled, letting the breath wash over my worried thoughts. Darius was right. At least he was alive. "Did anyone figure out what happened to him? Why was he stealing packages?"

The Conversationalists tutted and shook their heads. George did the same. Sometimes the ghosts knew more than the living residents of the building. But it seemed like we were all equally uninformed about this situation.

"We'll let you know the moment we hear anything, Nutmeg," Art said with a wave, probably noting my fatigued state.

"Bye, Conversationalists." I twiddled my fingers at them, noting the delighted expressions wash over each of their faces.

Art and Darius, especially, loved it when people used the name they'd coined for themselves.

Nancy's door was open as I walked toward the stairwell. The delicious scents of cranberries, orange, and cinnamon I'd noted yesterday wafted out once more to greet me.

"Nutmeg, you hungry?" Nancy's voice spilled out of the apartment.

I stopped, unsure how she'd known I was there since I couldn't see her. But I stepped closer to the threshold. "Always," I called inside.

She chuckled and stepped into my line of sight, holding a muffin toward me. "Here you go, doll. There's a dash of nutmeg in there, just for you." Her shrewd Nancy stare washed over me, and she added, "You all right?"

Forcing a smile, I said, "Just a long day. Much better now. Thanks, Nance." I held up the muffin in some sort of one-sided cake "cheers" as I made for the stairs.

Once I was on the fifth floor, my gaze traveled to the other side of the hallway, toward my friend Zoe's apartment. I reminded myself to text her and check in. She'd been nervous about the vacation in the mountains with her newly discovered family, the Stimacs.

At the end of the hallway, Mrs. Feldner's door opened. The tall guy that stepped out was definitely *not* the hunched-over, elderly Edna Feldner, however.

Taylor leaned out of her great-grandmother's apartment, kissing the guy as he braced himself in the doorway. He wore ripped jeans slung low on his hips and looked like at least one of his jobs might be listed as "DJ." I didn't see why they needed to make out in the hallway and couldn't help the tut of disapproval that spilled from my mouth. The teen's eyes flashed open, and she fixed me with an annoyed sneer. I quickly turned toward my apartment, unlocking it, and slipping inside with my muffin.

Ripley sat on the couch with Anise. She glanced up. "What are you hiding from?"

"Taylor and her boyfriend." I shook out my arms. "She scares me."

Ripley laughed. "She's nineteen."

Eyes wide, I said, "Yes, and somehow whenever I'm around her, I feel eighty-four instead of twenty-four."

"I'm guessing you got the job since you were gone a lot longer than you thought."

I ducked out from under my bag. "Yes, I also heard Julian's still in the coma. You get anything more than that from the hospital staff?"

"Nope." She wrinkled her nose. "I hung around for most of the morning, but when nothing seemed to be changing, I split."

My eyebrows rose. "Oh? Where'd you go?" She hadn't come to see me at the theatre, even though she'd said she wanted to be there with me.

"Uh, I had some other stuff to take care of," was all she divulged.

At a different time in our relationship, I might've pushed Ripley about the secrets she was obviously keeping from me. But ever since the summer, when she'd decided she wanted to start researching why she might still be here and how she might move on someday, the disappearances and secrets had become almost normal. I knew she'd tell me when she was ready. I took a bite of my muffin and plopped next to her on the couch.

"So..." She folded her feet underneath her. "Did you find out anything good? Do you think one of them tried to kill Winnie?"

Widening my eyes while I chewed the food in my mouth, I swallowed. "Oh, for sure. You should come with me tomorrow. It's wild there. *Bad* energy."

"But good enough for you to get the job," Ripley countered.

I tilted my head to one side. "Sure. I suppose. Oh, the biggest revelation is that Winnie isn't an actor. She works in the lighting-and-sound booth."

Ripley's red lips parted. "No way."

"Way." I took another bite of the delicious muffin. "The cast basically fought all day; that is, when the director wasn't yelling at everyone. He's a spitter."

"Like...?"

"When he talks—well, yells—he spits." I used my fingers to mime a spray coming from my mouth.

"Gross." Ripley stuck out her tongue in a gag.

"You want to know what's *not* gross?" My eyes lit up. "Damien. He's this beautiful, broody, backstage guy who could probably be on a magazine cover, but they've got him stuck behind the curtain."

"Hotter than Laurie?" Ripley asked, her dark eyes narrowing on me.

I reared away from her. "Psh, no way. Laurie's the full package. As far as I can tell, Damien is just a pretty face that can merely grunt and groan."

"And you think he's a suspect?" Ripley asked warily.

I rolled my shoulders. "I mean, he is very angry, and broody, but doesn't seem like the poisoning type."

Ripley's wary expression flattened. "Megs, have I taught you nothing?"

Flinching at her biting tone, I focused on my muffin, taking another bite. "Wut?" I asked guiltily through a full mouth.

"Hot people commit crimes too. Just because a man is attractive..." She circled her hands in front of her, waiting for me to finish the statement.

"That doesn't mean he doesn't have bodies in his basement," I said dejectedly, upset with myself for letting Damien's good looks trick me into lowering my guard.

Ripley shot me a sidelong glance. "Plenty of people thought Ted Bundy was handsome, and we *all* know how that turned out."

"Okay, broody Damien is definitely a suspect," I amended. "To be honest, they all are. Carter yells all the time, and even though Yasmine convinced him to hire me on the spot, she wouldn't make eye contact with me the rest of the day. Imogen doesn't seem to know anyone exists but herself, and there's some mysterious owner of the theatre that I'm going to meet soon." I slapped my hand down onto my leg. "Oh, there are also at least two ghosts. But I didn't get a chance to talk to them, not that they seemed to like me any more than the living people did."

Ripley looked like she was personally offended that anyone wouldn't like me. "These people sound like they're the worst."

It felt good to laugh. "They kind of are. But the theatre is charming, and I've got some fun ideas about what to paint for some of the props."

"Remember that you're searching for a possible murderer, though," Ripley warned.

Anise, who'd obviously crawled into Ripley's "lap" to sit with her—even though she just sank right through her—blinked up at Ripley's hands. It still weirded me out to think that Anise could see her or sense her spirit, at least to some degree. It wasn't a huge surprise, though. Cats always seemed to see things other animals didn't.

"I know." I glanced down at my lap. "Though, Winnie didn't seem so happy to see—"

The sound of my apartment buzzer cut me off. I held a finger up to Ripley and jogged over to check who it was.

When I opened the door, Laurie stood on the other side. He used his forearm to lean on my doorway much like Taylor's trendy boyfriend had been doing at 5D earlier. Suddenly, I understood the appeal.

"Hey." The smile I gave him was wide and unwieldy.

His lips crept up as his eyes locked on to me. "I came by to see how it went today. Sorry, I would've been here sooner, but just because they let me come home for a while doesn't mean they lightened my workload at all."

"That's okay. I actually just got back too." I tilted my head. "I got the job at the theatre, and I ended up staying most of the day while they went through rehearsal."

"Any chance you want to try again with the dinner we got waylaid from last night?" He jerked his head to the right.

Behind me, Ripley let out a little squeal of excitement. I

turned around for a split second and widened my eyes at my friend before facing Laurie again. "Uh, yeah. I'd love that," I said, not even catching my slip until Laurie craned his neck to look around me.

"Did you just check with your cat to make sure you could go on a date with me?" he asked through a grin.

When I looked back at the couch, Ripley grimaced and mouthed the word "Sorry," Anise still curled up with her. From Laurie's perspective, it probably *had* looked like I'd checked with the cat.

I laughed it off. "She's not used to me being gone all day. I just wanted to make sure she seemed okay. Which she does. Let me just grab my jacket."

Laurie stepped back as I slipped into my jacket and plucked my purse from its hook on the wall. As I pulled the door closed behind me, I glanced once more at my best friend, a huge smile on my face.

Ripley curled her fingers into excited fists, shaking them in front of her as she called out, "A date! Finally."

Seven

Laurie's hand settled on the small of my back as we walked toward the stairwell. My fingers tightened around the strap of my purse, the excess energy from my excitement needing somewhere to release.

"So, what was the Third Avenue like?" He held the door open for me, and I walked through, though not without missing his hand touching me.

"Confusing," I answered honestly. "It's old and cute, but it has a weird vibe."

"Anyone seem like they could've been the one to send her those chocolates?" he asked, repeating the questions I'd gotten from the Conversationalists upon my return.

Laughing again, though with much less humor, I said, "Yeah, like, all of them. Everyone there ranges from cranky and secretive to downright mean and ragey."

"Ragey?" Laurie chuckled.

I gave him a wide-eyed, *you have no idea* look before turning my attention back toward the stairs. "The director's main communication style is yelling with a side of insults. The actors seem self-absorbed, but also spent the day fighting with each other with an intensity I've rarely experienced. Even the lady that sells tickets and concessions is rude. Everyone else on the cast and crew wouldn't even make eye contact with me."

We reached the bottom of the stairwell, and Laurie stretched around me to grab the door. "And you're sure you're okay working with these people? Because there are other ways we can learn about"—he checked in the lobby before saying—"what happened to Winnie. I don't want you to feel stuck just because Ronny couldn't get a part in the play."

Sharing an amused grin as we considered what his audition must've been like, we walked through the lobby.

"I think it'll be good for me, actually," I told him as we reached the front doors of the building, waving to the Conversationalists—and ignoring the eyebrow waggling and grins the old-timers gave us at the sight of us going out together. "The flapper girls and felines paintings I've been working on have been fun, but I think I'm ready to move on from those."

After the summer I had, crawling around in the Seattle Underground with the ghost of a flapper who my cat happened to be especially entranced with, I'd started painting flapper girls with various cats. The Cooler, a speakeasy down the block, had agreed to display and sell them for me. And while I'd sold a few at that point, my well of inspiration to paint in that specific vein was drying out.

Laurie motioned for me to walk toward the water. "That makes sense. What have you been painting lately?"

I couldn't help the grin that spread across my face as I said, "I'm having fun doing collage-style paintings with Seattle nineties' grunge." I didn't add that the girl with the dyed red hair, black tights, boots, and flannel who often appeared in the paintings was my best friend instead of someone I'd made up based on pictures of the grunge scene from that time.

As I talked, Laurie reached forward and grabbed my hand, threading his fingers through mine, and directing me to cross the street with him. "Sounds great. You always did have a soft spot for that music."

At first, I thought the hand-holding might've been a nonverbal way to direct me where to go without interrupting as I explained my newest artistic inspiration, but he kept his hand locked with mine as we reached the other side of the street. I scooted closer, appreciating the hint of spiced cologne wafting off him.

"And your work?" I asked. "How are you feeling about staying over in Japan for another month or so?"

He swallowed, pulling us to a stop. "That's actually one of the things I wanted to talk to you about tonight."

I stared into his brown eyes, searching for answers. He angled his head to the right. We stood in front of a restaurant. I hadn't even realized we'd arrived at our destination.

"Oh, sure." I blinked. "This looks great."

He beamed. "It's pasta, and I know how you feel about carbs." He led me inside, giving the host his name.

Laurie had called in a reservation.

"That sure I was going to say yes to a date, huh?" I whispered teasingly over my shoulder as we trailed after the host through the small, dimly lit restaurant.

Laurie leaned down so his lips were close to my ear. "Let's call it more hopeful than sure."

My knees weakened at his nearness. Luckily, our host gestured to a table to my right, and I was able to sink into a chair before I truly lost my balance and things got embarrassing.

We spent the next few minutes being constantly bothered by the server, who asked questions about drinks and appetizers before listing a whole novel's worth of specials. When he came back almost immediately with the bottle of wine we ordered, annoyance flared in me. I wanted time alone with Laurie to figure out what he'd alluded to outside, and I couldn't do that when this server was being so attentive. I used the time it took for the server to open the bottle of wine to figure out what I wanted to eat. I couldn't pass up the handmade ravioli, and Laurie decided on the risotto special.

After the server filled our wineglasses and took our food orders, we were finally alone. Laurie held his glass forward, and I clinked mine against it.

"To Thanksgiving," I said. "Without it, I'd have to go even longer between seeing you … in person."

Laurie's smile was warm as he clinked again. "To a date with the girl I've wanted to ask out for, oh, eighteen years." He squinted one eye before drinking.

I choked on the sip of wine I'd been taking. "You wanted to ask me out when you were seven?"

Laurie fiddled with his wineglass. "Well, that might've been an exaggeration, but it feels like forever."

"Why didn't you, then?" My eyebrows scrunched together. "Not when you were seven, but when we were teenagers. You were always dating someone else."

Laurie coughed. "To be honest? For a long time, I thought it would jeopardize our friendship. You were one of my best friends, growing up, Meg."

"Same," I said, a smile peeking through my confusion. "But you're not worried about that anymore?"

He swirled the wine in his glass. "I think I've grown up enough that I can trust that I won't mess things up with you."

Air burst from my nostrils in disbelief. "You? Mess things up? Yeah, right."

"See? You're the person who sees the best in me, always has. I'm not perfect, Meg, and I didn't want you to see the truth."

I considered how Ripley often reprimanded me for how perfect I believed Laurie to be. She argued that I held him up to unrealistic standards.

"You don't think I know the true you?" I asked seriously, worry softening my question.

"Sorry, that's not what I'm trying to say. I'm wording this poorly." He squeezed his eyes shut for a moment. "I meant that I don't think *I* truly knew who I was until recently. I thought you were wrong for liking me so much, for only seeing the good in me." He took a sip of wine like it was a lifeline. Before I could protest, he added, "But this summer, when we had that fight about Gavin's involvement in the

Elliott murder, I realized that you *do* see my flaws. You just respect me enough to give me the benefit of the doubt." His posture eased. "I *know* now that you see the true me, Meg. I think you're the person in my life who might know me the best, and I feel like I know you better than anyone."

I gulped, realizing I couldn't agree with him, because he didn't know everything there was to know about me. There was a very big secret I'd kept from him—and everyone else in my life. But Ripley and I had played out that conversation, and there never seemed to be a good, non-worrisome way to tell the people I love that I could commune with spirits. One thing at a time, I decided.

Reaching forward, I took his hand. "Well, I'm glad one of us finally worked up the courage. Thank you for asking me out."

His gaze traveled over me. "I still remember when you asked if I wanted to go to Flatstick Pub with you this summer, when you first moved home. I was in shock, I was so excited. And then I worried that you only asked me there because I'd been threatened by Mr. Miller's murderer."

So, Laurie's reaction to me admitting that was my reason for inviting him out that night hadn't been relief—as I'd feared—but disappointment that it wasn't a date. If I'd only been brave enough to tell him how I truly felt back then…

"Then, on the Fourth, it seemed like I hadn't actually been reading too much into things."

"You weren't," I assured him.

"*But* I'd gotten the call about Japan, and it didn't seem fair to make you wait for me." He winced. "It still doesn't, if I'm being honest."

"Laurie, I moved across the country for five years and I *still* couldn't stop thinking of you."

"Really?" His lips pulled into a striking smile.

Covering my face, I groaned as I admitted, "There's no one else. There never has been. I'll wait for you as long as it takes because I've been waiting all this time anyway."

Gentle fingers pried my hands from my face. Laurie's eyes practically sparkled in the dim candlelight of the restaurant. "It's always been you for me, Meg," he said.

And we might've kissed—I think—but the prompt server brought over our dinners at that exact moment. We shared an amused glance and dug in, taking tastes of one another's meals and moving on to less-intense topics as we ate.

"You know, I thought about trying to get a reservation for The Cooler," Laurie said once his plate was clean. "I really want to see your art for sale, and it sounded so fun. But I have to admit that I'm happy we got food. I think a dinner of purely cocktails would've been a bad idea, especially with the conversation I wanted to have."

I patted my stomach. "And since all I had for lunch was a muffin from Nancy on my way back from the theatre this afternoon. Plus, we should wait until Zoe's back from her vacation to go to The Cooler."

His eyes flared wider. "Yeah, I really want to meet her too. You said she's in the mountains?"

Chuckling preemptively, I said, "With her newly discovered family, the Stimacs. The ones who own the speakeasy and the bar above it."

"The ones you thought might be murderers this summer?" He cocked an eyebrow.

I ducked my chin. "They turned out not to be, and they've been nice to Zoe. She doesn't really have a family now that her mom is gone, and it turned out her dad died when she was a toddler. I told her she was welcome at the Morrisey Thanksgiving, but the Stimacs apparently rent out a cabin in the mountains for the whole week before, and she wanted to check it out, see if it was any fun."

"Makes sense." Laurie finished his wine. "And what about your plans for Thanksgiving? Would you like to come to mine? My parents would love to see you."

The invitation warmed me to my bones. "Thank you. I'd love to see your parents, but I've already committed to bringing the stuffing for the Morrisey dinner, and you know how Nancy hates last-minute changes."

He released a breathy laugh. "I do." Glancing down at the check, already paid and signed for, Laurie said, "Well, should we get going?"

I hooked my arm through his as we walked back to the Morrisey. Not wanting the night to end just yet, I went with him on a late-night walk with Leo down to the waterfront. And as he stopped at my apartment door after walking me "home" at the end of the night, Laurie kissed me.

For someone who'd spent far too long imagining what it might be like to kiss Laurie, I learned that my fantasies hadn't even come close to reality.

If I hadn't already been his, that first kiss would've sealed my fate.

Eight

"Okay, tell me again about the kiss." Ripley fanned herself like a Jane Austen heroine the next morning as I got ready for my day at the theatre.

Laughing, I said, "I already explained it in detail last night."

"I know," she whined. "But, Meg, this is *Laurie*. The love of your life." She moved like she was going to lean against the wall but simply fell through it.

For a moment my heart hurt, wishing Addy were here. Our nineteen twenties' ghostly friend would've loved to dish about boys with us if her spirit hadn't moved on. The pang of sadness turned into a deep ache as I thought about Ripley's efforts to figure out what unfinished business was holding her back from moving on as well. What would I do when she wasn't here to talk to either?

I schooled my expression back into one of concentration as I swiped mascara over my lashes. Ripley didn't notice my emotional stumble by the time she reemerged through the wall. Despite my earlier protests, she watched me expectantly, waiting to hear about my first kiss with Laurie again.

So, I indulged her. "The kiss was perfect, of course." I relived the whole thing one more time for my best friend.

Maybe our moments together would never end, and she'd be by my side forever, but if they were fleeting, I didn't want to miss out on a single one.

❦

ABOUT A HALF AN HOUR LATER, armed with a coffee and a snack for after, I walked up to the Third Avenue Theatre, feeling miles more prepared than I had been yesterday. I was also armed with my best friend today, which only added to my confidence.

"Okay, I can see it. Kind of the cute, run-down look." Ripley nodded her approval at the ivy-covered façade of the building.

Just having Ripley by my side made me stand taller and my strides longer. I knocked on the glass of the front doors just as I had yesterday, waiting for the cranky Francine to begrudgingly let me inside.

"Great, you're back," Francine said blandly, stringing out the words so they sounded ultra sarcastic.

"Dude, you weren't kidding." Ripley eyed the woman and then moved her assessment over the rest of the theatre. "There's a bad energy here."

Unable to respond to Ripley in front of Francine, I just tugged on my earlobe, our silent sign for yes. Instead of going to the stage today, however, I veered down the hallway to the left toward the prop room. Ripley chattered as we walked through the quiet hallway, verbally processing everything I'd told her yesterday about these people.

"So ... Imogen is the blonde who's playing Lina Lamont," she repeated. "And Yasmine is the knockout who's playing Kathy Selden. Damien is hot but possibly scary. Tony is forgettable, but somehow got the part of charismatic Cosmo. And the guy playing Don is actually named Don?"

"Correct," I whispered, stifling a giggle.

The fact that Ripley was a good listener was not news to me, but I was a little surprised that she'd remembered so much of what I'd talked about yesterday, even down to what the lead actors looked like.

"And this is me." I held my hands out to the door marked Props at the end of the hallway.

"Ahhh," Ripley said, impressed.

Until I opened the door, and we stepped foot inside the large storeroom that seemed to be a catchall for everything from costumes to old props and even someone's old toaster oven. I hadn't noticed what a junk collection it was yesterday, but I also hadn't been afforded a ton of time to look around, either, during Carter's whirlwind tour. Looking at it through my best friend's eyes was much more worrisome.

"Okay. All right." Ripley's tone wobbled as she appraised the space. "This is ... well, it sure is something." She bared her teeth in a smile.

I laughed. "I know it's terrible. You're not going to hurt my feelings."

"At least you have it to yourself," she said.

I wasn't 100 percent sure that I did. Carter's insistence

that Damien would be available to help me left me unclear about where he spent his time. A large barn-style sliding door led to the backstage area. Although it was closed now, it would probably be open during dress rehearsals and shows. Did Damien slip in and out of it during rehearsals? He'd been on call basically the whole time yesterday, but was that a one-time thing or an everyday occurrence?

Muffled music leaked through that door as did Carter's shrill directions to the actors. They'd already started for the day.

Ripley's gaze followed the sound, and she widened her eyes. "The director sounds just as pleasant as you described." She scooted closer to me, jabbing an elbow in my direction. "I haven't seen any of the ghosts yet. Was there one in here yesterday when you came through?"

Shivering, I nodded. This had been where I'd seen the regal woman with the flowing slacks and brown hair pulled into a smart bun.

"That bad?" Ripley asked, noting my reaction.

"Not bad, necessarily," I whispered, still unsure if we were alone. "But I got the distinct impression that she did not want to talk to me."

Ripley pursed her lips. "Maybe she didn't realize you could see her. You were with Carter, and she's likely not used to people noticing her presence."

"Normally, I would agree. But she and I locked eyes. I did a full double take." I cut the air with my hand. "She knew I saw her. She just didn't care."

"Huh." Ripley processed the information. "And you spotted another one too?"

"A man," I confirmed. "Out in the lobby by the bathrooms. He didn't pay attention to me, either, but *his* irreverence might've been because he didn't think I noticed him."

"By the bathrooms?" Her nose wrinkled. "You think he's some kind of peeper?"

Unable to say for sure one way or the other, I said, "Oh, gosh. Maybe. At least I'll be able to see him if he tries to do anything weird."

"You would, but no one else will." Ripley moved on quickly. "Okay, so what are we working on today?"

Slipping the list I'd made yesterday from my purse, I tapped the three items I'd circled. "I want to start with the flats I need to paint because they're the largest and will need time to dry. Once I have the basic shapes on those, I can move to painting the wooden sets. Most of the other stuff, I'll have to scrounge around here for or ask Damien to make me."

Eyes widening, Ripley said, "Right. I gotta see this guy who's so hot that he made you forget all the self-preservation wisdom Penny and I worked so hard to drill into you." She smirked when I sent her a glowering look. "After I do a little tour around the theatre, I'll search through all of this junk while you paint to see if I can't help you find some of the stuff on your list."

Any irritation I'd felt at her comment about Damien immediately lessened with her offer to help wade through the piles of junk back here. "Thanks."

She disappeared, and I located the paint Carter or Damien had set aside for me. They'd already set up three flats for me against the wall. I wondered if Damien was going to have to try his hand at the paintings if I hadn't arrived. If that were the case, one would think the man would be a little nicer to me. I'd saved him from having to do this himself.

I got to work, simultaneously intimidated by the large scale of the paintings but loving the challenge. I did a basic outline using pencil and then got started on laying down the big swaths of color needed for the base. While I painted, I kept an eye out for the ghosts I'd seen yesterday. But Ripley was the only ghost I'd encountered by the time she returned from her private tour of the theatre.

"You were *not* joking." She fanned her face. "Damien is volcanic."

Still holding on to the paintbrush, I opened my palms as much as possible. "See? I told you."

She gave me a pointed look. "But super broody, and definitely capable of killing. Something about those ice-blue eyes."

"I can't tell if you're scared or in love."

"Me neither." She scrunched her nose and then shook her head as if clearing it of those thoughts. "Okay, where's that list of yours?"

I jabbed my paintbrush over to the stool I'd left the list on.

Ripley, who never did anything quietly, narrated as she searched through the props and costumes.

"They must've done *Cats!* at some point, because there are a lot of tails over here."

I giggled.

"Oh, I saw your two ghosts," she called from behind the two-dimensional wooden cutout of a car.

"Yeah?" Interest stilled my hand. "They talk to you?"

"Not a peep. I even waved. They're pretty transparent. I wondered if they thought I was still living, and that's why they wouldn't speak to me either."

We'd encountered ghosts that had such anger and resentment toward living people that they wouldn't deign to talk to me, despite my unique ability to help them figure out why they were still here and possibly move on.

Ripley continued her story. "So I walked straight through a wall to prove I was one of them, but they still wouldn't even look at me."

"Maybe they're snobs," I guessed aloud.

A derisive snort came from behind me, and I checked over my shoulder. I jolted as I found the brown-haired ghost from yesterday. She was looking down her nose at me, both literally and figuratively.

About to apologize for my comment, a crashing noise over in the corner startled me. When I turned to look for the ghost behind me again, she was gone.

"Hey. Careful, Rip. You just scared away one of the theatre ghosts. She seemed like she was going to talk to me." The words slashed out of me, harsh and cutting. I jolted at the surge of anger toward Ripley, unsure where it had come from or why I'd been so quick to irritation when my normal inclination would've been to check on her well-being.

"Sorry," Ripley called, sounding far away. "I'm okay, by the way. Thanks for asking." The words came out slower than they normally would, only adding to my irritation.

Instead of snapping at her again, I asked, "You sure?" I mean, obviously she was. She didn't have a body to hurt, but the question was more one of habit. "What are you trying to move?"

Most ghosts had the ability to manipulate the physical world to a certain, rudimentary extent, using bursts of energy. The use of that energy had a consequence Ripley referred to as "going sketchy." She would turn transparent for a while after, and her words would come out elongated and slow, like she was trying to talk under water.

"Just a teensy bit sketchy," Ripley replied. "It was worth it, though. I found you a couch for the scene where they sing 'Good Morning.'"

My frustration at losing out on a chance to talk to the theatre ghost ebbed. "Thanks," I muttered, slightly embarrassed by my outburst. I went back to painting.

The time flew by as I lost myself in my work. Ripley located a few more items on my list, thankfully without having to use any more of her energy to move anything. Sounds of the rehearsal happening on the other side of the stage door acted as the background. Lines, music, and Carter's yelling melded together.

It wasn't until a few hours later that there was a break in the sounds coming from the stage. Standing and brushing off my overalls, I surveyed my work so far. The scene was the interior of a house. It was the simplest of the flats Carter had asked for, so I decided to tackle it first.

"Brilliant, as always." Ripley tipped her head forward in appreciation. "You done with this one?"

I dunked the paintbrush I'd been using in the cup of water, sloshing it around as I rotated my head to see the painting from a different angle. "I'm not sure. But I want to let it sit for a bit before I add anything else. I want to use this break they're having to talk to Winnie again."

Ripley's eyes lit up at the suggestion. "Oh, good idea."

Wiping off my hands as well as I could, Ripley and I made the trip to the light booth. I didn't want to chance running into Carter and him adding to my list or eating up all my time during the break, so I opted to head out into the lobby and climb the stairs to the lighting booth from that direction.

While the rest of the cast and crew seemed to be taking a lunch break, Winnie was frantically searching for something in the space under her desk that held the patchboard and controls. She was muttering to herself, though I couldn't make out what exactly she was saying.

I didn't want to startle her, but the longer I stood there without her noticing, the more surprising it was going to be. So, I cleared my throat.

Winnie jumped, hitting her head and letting out a yowl. Her eyes snapped over to me as she rubbed at the back of her skull.

"Oh, it's you." The words were neither dramatic nor mean, just flat.

"Yeesh. Even Winnie's worse here," Ripley muttered.

"Winnie," I said, walking forward, keeping my voice down just in case they could hear us from the stage. "You need my help. Someone sent those chocolates to you, and I have a bad feeling it's someone here."

"Of course it is. These people are all terrible," she said, not lowering her voice in the least, obviously not worried by the idea that they might hear.

"Why didn't you admit as much to the police, then?"

She was agitated. Her scarf was so much longer on one side that it was barely hanging on, and her normally braided hair was falling forward into her face.

I peered at her. "Unless you already know who it was?"

"I don't. But even if I did, what are *you* going to do about it?"

"Megs here has solved three murders since she's been back in Seattle." Ripley narrowed her eyes at our neighbor.

Not in the mood to convince Winnie of my qualifications, I simply said, "I'm going to help you, be another set of eyes and ears here."

Pursing her lips, pinching them to one side of her face, then the other, Winnie finally exhaled. "Fine. You can help me."

"What changed?" Ripley asked.

That question I *would* repeat. "What made you reconsider?"

Winnie huffed. "Well, it's not like you're going anywhere. I also don't particularly believe you're going to find anything, so ... be my guest."

It wasn't exactly an endorsement, but it was better than what I'd gotten yesterday. I would have to take it.

"Deal. Any ideas where I should start looking? Anyone here you think might've wanted you dead?" I asked.

Hope spurred inside my chest as Winnie moved aside a purple folder, picked up a folded piece of paper, and handed it over.

It was a program for the upcoming production of *Singing in the Rain.*

"What am I supposed to do with this?" I asked, deadpan.

She jerked her chin toward the program. "There's the list of people you should look into."

"All of them?" I suppressed the urge to bang my head against the wall.

Winnie merely nodded.

Nine

I released an abrupt puff of air. "Winnie, you cannot be serious. The whole cast and crew has reason to want you dead?"

"If you can't handle it, you can quit and leave me alone." Her tone held a challenge.

"What was she looking for just now? Under her desk?" Ripley asked, craning her neck to see where Winnie had been searching when we'd arrived.

I repeated the question.

"Oh, I dropped a chocolate under here earlier, and I don't want it to melt into the carpet." She frowned at the dark space under the patchboard.

Ripley and I shared a skeptical look.

"Are you sure it's safe to be eating chocolates?" I ventured.

Winnie let out an exasperated snort. "Don't worry. I bought the chocolate. There's no way I'm eating anything that comes in the mail." She crossed her arms. Well, she tried, but her long silk scarf got in the way, so she wrestled with it until she got it out from under her arm and then wound it around her neck. "So? Is that all?"

I blinked. "Of course not!" Gripping the program tighter to vent some of my frustration, I shook it in the air. "Do you really expect me to question every person here?"

"They all have a reason to want me dead. They're all jealous, vain, and corrupt."

"They should use that to advertise working here," Ripley scoffed.

Humoring Winnie, mostly because I didn't have the energy to fight her, I looked at the list. Imogen Sharpe's name was listed first. Tapping the page, I asked, "What about Imogen? What does she have against you?"

Winnie wafted over to her chair and sank into it. "That vain excuse for a leading lady accused me of lighting her poorly on purpose, making her look older than she is."

"Not really something to kill over, but okay," Ripley muttered.

I was about to ask why that would be so bad, when Winnie said, "The critic who was here that night wrote about it in the piece he published. He ripped her apart. I think he even mentioned that it looked like she was growing a mustache." Winnie had the sense to flinch at repeating that comment.

I still wasn't sure how that qualified as reason to kill someone, but it also didn't sound like the first run in those two had. I moved on to Yasmine Zara. According to Winnie, Yasmine had hated her ever since she started working there five years ago because Winnie was always turning down her microphones. Winnie argued that it was because she was constantly too pitchy, and the fighting continued during every other production they'd done together since.

We went through the whole cast and crew like that, including Damien, Carter, Tony, and Don. But when I got to Francine, listed under the ticket-and-concession booth area, Winnie stiffened.

"Don't bother with Francine. The chocolates weren't from her." Winnie's eyes cut to the side and she swallowed.

I was about to push when Carter's voice boomed through the auditorium. "Okay, people. Lunch is over. Let's get back to work."

"Sorry you didn't get to eat." I took a step away from her.

"I'm not like the dancing puppets out there," Winnie said. "I can eat whenever I want." As if to prove that fact, she pulled a lunchbox from the drawer of her desk and zipped it open.

With that, Ripley and I turned to leave.

"That was suspicious," Ripley said as we walked back through the lobby toward the hallway.

"Tell me about it," I whispered, letting my focus linger on the concession stand where Francine usually stood. She wasn't there, so we slipped down the hallway, retreating to the sanctuary of junk while the cast filtered back onto the stage.

With Ripley by my side, I already expected not to be the only soul in the prop room. My sighting of the female ghost earlier had even prepared me for the possibility of more than the two of us. But I hadn't expected to find one of the cast members standing in front of the flat I'd been working on all morning as I entered.

Her blonde hair was pinned up, and she was still wearing her fancy gown from the movie premiere scene.

"Hi. Imogen, was it?" My voice was small, mostly because I didn't want to scare the woman by sneaking up on her.

She didn't jump or whirl around, proving she'd heard me approaching. But she also didn't tear her attention away from the large canvas.

Gut clenching in fear that it looked bad or that she might've touched it when it was still drying, I stepped up next to her.

"This is really amazing," she said, settling my worries even as I scanned the piece to confirm that it was okay.

Pride expanded in my chest. "Thank you."

Imogen finally glanced up at me. "No. I'm serious. We've never had someone so talented working in props as long as I've been here. It's beautiful." Her voice was musical and pretty in real life, holding none of the nasal, shrieking quality it did as she played Lina Lamont.

I met her striking hazel eyes and smiled. "It's been a lot of fun so far."

Imogen looked around at the storage room, then let her eyelids slide closed for a moment. She inhaled, deep and long. "Sorry to intrude on your space, I just needed a little peace and quiet."

As if on cue, Carter yelled, "Damien, that curtain better not be in that position again during this scene."

"Aren't they going to miss you?" I jabbed a thumb toward the stage.

She swung her head back and forth. "I'm not in this scene. I have about"—she checked her watch—"another ten minutes of freedom, if I'm guessing correctly about the number of times Carter's going to make them rerun their lines."

As if he heard her, Carter bellowed, "Nope. Do that again."

Imogen's shoulders dropped a further few millimeters in relief.

Ripley pointed at the program in my hand, the one I'd clutched ever since leaving Winnie's booth. She was right. This was a perfect time to question the woman, but I hesitated, hating to ruin what little quiet time Imogen had away from the stage with a bunch of questions.

Still, there was a chocolate poisoning murderer on the loose. That had to take precedence.

"So, it seems like you all know each other pretty well around here. How long have you been rehearsing this play?" I focused on my painting, noting a few areas where I wanted to add more color and depth to the scene to make it look more three-dimensional.

Imogen exhaled a quick laugh. "It seems like forever, but in reality, it's only been a few weeks. We have a lot of the same cast for each musical we do, though, so that's why it might seem like we've known each other for a long time."

"Oh? I thought theatres usually brought in new cast and directors for each production."

"Usually places do. The bigger theatres do. But we're so

small—and we don't have many people auditioning—so we end up having a lot of the same cast each time." She wobbled her head from side to side. "With the exception of a few parts here and there."

I couldn't help but spare a thought for Ronny, who didn't even make the cut at a theatre that seemed almost desperate for new actors.

"And Carter?" I asked as he bellowed again from the stage. "Is he always the director?"

"Despite the fact that he quits after each production and says he's never working with any of us again, yes, he always comes back." She cleared her throat. "Again, not the usual way things are done, but it's how Petra works. And really, Carter's not so bad. He's loud, but he gets results. He's louder the closer we are to opening night. During casting and table reads, he's a lot calmer."

Fingers itching to fix a slight discoloration that caught my eye on the flat I had been painting, I grabbed a brush and dipped it in the paint as I asked her, "And what about Winnie? She's interesting."

It seemed likely that Winnie was even more close-lipped here than she was at the Morrisey with details about her life. I was banking on her not having told anyone I was from her building.

Imogen rolled her eyes. "That's an understatement."

"Is she at least good at her job?"

The blonde squinted one eye. "She's better at it than Francine."

"Francine?"

"She used to have that job," Imogen said. "But Winnie

convinced Petra to give it to her instead, and Francine got moved to tickets and concessions, which she hates."

Ripley and I exchanged a pointed glance.

"Why do you ask?" Imogen narrowed her eyes, but then she added, "Do you want her job? Based on what I've already seen, you'd probably be better at it than her." She chuckled.

I joined in with a laugh, though it came out a little more nervous sounding than I'd hoped. "No, I just know lighting and sound can make or break a show, and she seems ... unpredictable."

"You're not wrong about the first part. Lighting can make even the prettiest person look like a mess." Imogen twirled her blonde hair around a manicured finger.

Ripley made a throat-clearing sound and leaned closer. "Is that so?"

"But Winnie isn't unpredictable," Imogen added before I could say anything. "She has messed up in the past, but she learns from her mistakes and tries to be better each show, which is more than I can say for Yasmine."

From the evenness of her tone, Imogen didn't sound like someone who was harboring hatred for Winnie. In fact, she didn't even sound upset with the woman, let alone like someone who might want to kill her.

Francine, on the other hand ... Imogen had made it sound like she and Winnie were mortal enemies. Odd, considering that Winnie had told me not to bother looking into her.

"Sorry, I shouldn't have said that about Yasmine. Honestly, I'm usually a big champion of other women. We've got to stick together in a tough industry like this."

Over the intercom system, Damien's deep voice called for Imogen to report to the stage.

She smiled weakly. "I guess ten minutes was a generous guess. That's my cue." With a wave, she was gone.

"That definitely sounds like Francine *is* worth questioning," Ripley said once we were alone.

"Tell me about it. Winnie stole her job right out from under her." I washed out the brush and dipped it in a brown, adding dimension to the doorframe I'd painted in the scene. Finishing up that color, I stood and inclined my head in appreciation. "I think I'm done fussing over it now." Setting down the paintbrush, I looked at Ripley. "Should we see if we can find Francine and question her?"

Ripley held up a finger. "She wasn't there a few minutes ago. I'll check, so you don't have to walk all the way down there."

Thanking my friend before she disappeared, I got to work cleaning out the brushes and sealing up the paints. I crossed the first flat off the list and contemplated the other two I needed to paint. My gaze wandered over to the large wooden structure Damien had already built for the street scenes. Immediately, an idea came to me for a way to texture the bricks on the buildings. While my mind was deep in a creative thought process, Ripley appeared, causing me to jump.

She frowned. "No Francine at the ticket desk or anywhere in the lobby. I even checked the bathroom," she whispered.

"Look who's the peeper now," I said with a chuckle.

"Please." Ripley fixed me with a poison-tipped look. "I

meant that I looked for shoes under the stall doors. She wasn't in there. Yasmine was, though. She was on the phone, talking about how gross she thinks Don is."

"Oh?"

That was news to me. The scenes I'd witnessed them in together yesterday had made them look like they were positively in love. She must be a really great actor.

Nodding toward the large wooden structure in the back, I said, "No rush on finding Francine. I'm going to start painting the buildings. Will you keep an eye out for her and let me know if she reappears?"

Ripley's eyes sparkled. "Will do." And with that, I was alone again.

As much as I enjoyed the songs in the musical, Carter's yelling was too much to handle while I was trying to be creative. I pulled my earbuds out of my bag and turned on some music. Then I got started on the buildings, loving how the technique I'd thought up just minutes before translated into textured-looking bricks.

"I think I need to paint on giant surfaces all the time," I told myself.

Ripley showed up a while later.

"Did you find Francine?" I asked.

"I think she's gone home. Everyone else is heading that way too. They're all in their changing rooms getting ready to leave."

Air slipped down my throat as I sucked in a surprised breath. I checked the clock on my phone and realized I'd been painting for hours. The time had flown by, and with my music playing, I hadn't heard the rehearsal end.

"Well, we can catch her tomorrow." I turned to clean up.

"I may not have found Francine, but I didn't come away from my snooping empty-handed," Ripley said, a teasing lilt to her voice, as if the information she'd learned was a physical object she was dangling in front of me.

"Oh?" I asked, continuing my cleanup.

"There are *three* ghosts haunting this theatre."

"Three?" Okay, that got me to turn around.

"The brunette is named Katherine. There's a blonde named Janet, and the peeper's name is Nathanial. The weirdest part? None of them can leave this building."

"How'd you find out all that?" I placed a hand on my hip, careful not to get more paint on my overalls than was already there.

Ripley squinted one eye. "I may have talked to the peeper. I also have to take back the whole peeper comment. He doesn't seem like a creep. He's a former director here. He says he hangs out in the lobby because his favorite thing was to listen to the audience chat about the show during intermission and after the play."

Laughing, I said, "Well, I'm glad he gave you the time of day. I couldn't even get him to acknowledge me."

"He didn't want to talk to me at first either. And, when I told him about you, and how you can see us, he told me they 'don't talk to *livings* around here.'" Despite the absolute venom in her voice when she used his derogatory term for me, Ripley's eyes sparkled. "But then I found his weakness."

I cocked an eyebrow.

"Insulting the directing skills of Carter," she said with a feral grin.

Neither the statement nor that look were like my friend. Ripley could be blunt, sure, but not usually mean. She loved to bask in the antics of our Morrisey neighbors, but she wasn't one to pick people apart. If the worry I felt at her statement so much as flitted across my face, Ripley didn't notice. She kept going, bragging about her conversation with the other ghost.

"I found him hovering at the open door to the auditorium, mumbling about how Carter was doing everything wrong. I agreed with him, profusely, and we had a long conversation about the cast. He's the one who told me about Janet. I still haven't seen her. Apparently, she likes to hide up on the catwalk."

I pushed past my reservations surrounding Ripley tearing apart Carter's directing skills to gain favor with the other ghost and focused on the part of her story to do with Janet.

"Interesting. Was she a backstage worker?" I asked, wondering why she'd be drawn to that area. I hadn't seen any spirits on the catwalk when Carter had given me the tour. Then again, I had been running.

Ripley shook her head. "Katherine and Janet were both actresses."

"Huh." I cleaned my brush in the water and set it aside to dry. Surveying the prop room, I decided everything looked cleaned up enough for me to go home for the evening.

"Let's walk through the stage on our way out," I told Ripley. "I want to see if we can't catch a glimpse of this Janet character. If Janet's around the stage a lot, she might've overheard one of the actors threatening Winnie."

But before we could leave the prop room, a loud *BOOM*

ricocheted off the walls. The floors shook with the impact of whatever had fallen on the stage.

We were moving before either of us could say a thing, taking the first left, toward the stage. The first thing that caught my eye was a person standing on the stage. She was obviously a ghost, given her translucent state, and she was blonde, as Ripley had described. But she was standing over something, looking down at it in disgust.

I moved closer. "Janet?"

The ghost's gaze traveled up to the catwalk. "I think someone is up there." Her eyes narrowed and then she vanished.

The shape lying on the stage remained, however, and it quickly became clear that it was a person. Not a ghost. This person was alive—or *had* been until recently, I realized as I moved closer.

Crumpled lifelessly on the stage was Francine. A light lay next to her, and a pool of blood surrounded her head.

Ten

It wasn't as if I was looking at my first dead body. Not by a long shot. But the sight of Francine lying motionless on the stage hit me differently somehow.

"Well, looks like we missed our opportunity to question Francine," Ripley said.

Ripley's words felt like a punch to the gut, not only because they were morbid as all get out, but because they were also true. We'd missed our chance.

I was about to wheel on her, to scold her for such an insensitive statement, when footsteps pounded through the theatre. Worried voices filled the lobby as the cast and crew came racing through the house doors, sliding to a collective stop as they saw Francine's body—saw the stage light and the blood pooling.

"What's going on here?" Carter elbowed his way through the crowd. His face was pinched with annoyance, as if he were calculating how much of a setback that loud of a noise was going to cost him and the show.

I clocked the exact moment his gaze landed on Francine. He lurched forward, dry heaving as he clung to the back of the wooden bench seating.

"Call nine-one-one," I snapped at the gawking group.

No one moved. Their attention, however, narrowed on me, on where I'd been standing—closest to the stage. Paranoia flared inside my chest, tightening like restrictive hands closing around my throat. Did they think I had something to do with what happened to Francine?

"Fine. I'll call," I said, pulling out my phone and dialing the three numbers.

Imogen broke away from the group and tottered toward Carter while I spoke to the dispatcher. She settled a gentle hand on his shoulder. By the time I'd hung up the call, her hazel eyes pooled with tears. "What an awful accident," she said.

"Accident," Carter repeated. The word was a ghost of his usual yelled-communication style.

And it calmed me as much as it seemed to settle Carter. Accident. This had been an accident. My paranoia was likely unwarranted. No one thought I had done anything to hurt Francine. A stage light had fallen on her in a freak accident. Why had my mind gone to murder right away?

Ripley reappeared by my side, making me jump. I hadn't even clocked that she'd left while I talked to the dispatcher. I put my phone back to my ear, so anyone who saw me might think I was still on the phone with emergency services.

"Where have you been?" I whispered toward the wall so the others wouldn't hear me.

Ripley flinched at the bite in my question. Her hands

came up between us. "Just asking Janet what she meant by that cryptic thing she said about someone being on the catwalk."

Right. *That* was why I hadn't immediately ruled the scene as an accident. "And, did you? Get her to explain?"

"No." Ripley huffed, hugging her arms tight around her middle. "She just said there was a sound."

"Well, duh. We all heard the sound." I couldn't seem to dull the sharpness in my tone, the sarcasm lacing my words.

Ripley met my attitude with even more of her own. "She meant on the catwalk. The light was already on the stage," she scoffed as if I were being dense on purpose.

The reminder cut me down a notch. "Surely it was just a piece of metal or wire moving in the wake of the light falling. Right?" Worry iced its way down my spine as I gulped, hoping Ripley would agree with me.

When she didn't, I looked over at the group of actors huddled together in misery. Tears fell, shoulders shook as they cried, gasps cleaved the air as they took breaths in between their sobs. They all looked so terribly sad. They grieved so perfectly, it was almost as if I were watching a scene from a play.

Had one of them dropped that light on Francine? Suddenly, Imogen's use of the word *accident* didn't sit so well. I dropped my phone away from my ear, tucking it into my purse.

Sirens blared in front of the theatre. Emergency vehicles screeched to a halt, taking up the street parking in front of the building. The gathered cast filed into the rows of audience seating so the main walkways would be clear as a flood of people rushed in. Damien stood in the lobby, having opened the doors for the EMTs.

Because Francine wasn't here to unlock them anymore.

"We just found her like this about five minutes ago. A stage light fell on her head," Imogen explained as the first responders swept past her.

Ripley followed the group as they worked their way over to the stage. Police streamed in after the paramedics, and Imogen filled them in just as she'd done with the first group. Gratitude for Ripley and Imogen overcame me. Hopefully, Ripley would be able to learn something helpful by hanging out near the first responders. And seeing as my hands were shaking, and I couldn't get my thoughts in order, I was glad Imogen had stepped up as our ambassador with the EMTs. I wasn't in a state to coherently explain anything. She was obviously a person who was able to keep her cool during an emergency. I certainly was not such a person.

Neither was Carter, it seemed.

"Stage light." He ground out the two words, his face setting in a terrifying glare. His phone was in out of his pocket in an instant, and he paced down the row of seats. He only held it to his ear for a moment before yelling, "Wisteria, get yourself back to the theatre. Now." There was fire in his eyes as he listened. "I don't care if you just got home. Francine is dead, and it's your fault." This time, he didn't wait to hear what she had to say in response. He ended the call and made another. "You're going to need to come down to the theatre. We have a big problem." Despite the words he used being very similar to the ones he'd said to Winnie, his tone was much less demanding with whomever he'd called the second time. Carter ended that call as well, and then stalked through the house doors.

Still on the stage, Ripley leaned in to hear more of what the police were saying. She kept enough distance that she wasn't in the way; her hatred for having a living person walk through her overriding at least some of her curiosity. After a few minutes, she returned to my side.

"They're not as convinced that it was an accident, so they're going to question everyone who was here," she told me.

Hearing that they were going to look into it settled my nerves. Their doubt also made me think back to what Janet had said about the catwalk. I could always tell the police that *I'd* heard the sound above. I was the first one on the scene after all. No one would be able to say I was lying. But I didn't know Janet at all. Was she sure about what she'd heard? Maybe she was always hearing things. I didn't want to send the police on a wild-goose chase just because I took the word of a random ghost.

Resigned to let Janet's comment go, for now, I slid my phone from my purse. I opened a note and typed out a message to Ripley, knowing I wouldn't be able to talk to her with so many people around.

Carter called Winnie. She was already home. He also called someone else.

Her eyebrows lifted. "I guess we'll find out who, soon."

I erased what I'd written before and replaced it with a question. **No Detective Anthony?**

"The officers didn't mention her specifically," Ripley

said. "But they mentioned forensics is sending whatever personnel they can afford. They should be here soon."

Well, the detective *had* told Winnie they were swamped. Movement by the door closest to the prop room caught my eye. The brunette ghost stood there, staring at the scene. Katherine, Ripley had called her. I typed out one last thing. **Can you ask the other two ghosts if they saw or heard anything? Maybe they can explain what Janet heard on the catwalk.**

Ripley followed my gaze. "I'll work on it." She was gone a moment after that.

I continued to watch the police work until one of the officers scanned the seats and called out, "Who was on the scene first?"

Raising my hand, I took one step forward. "It was me."

Behind me, the cast members whispered again, sparking that earlier feeling of paranoia. I reminded myself that I was the only one who had reason to think this might not be an accident. The cast members were merely shocked. They didn't suspect that I had anything to do with Francine's death.

The whispering died down, and I breathed easily once more. But as I checked over my shoulder, I caught two people still staring at me. Yasmine's dark brown eyes bore into me almost as palpably as Damien's ice-blue ones. Interesting. The two of them stood on opposite sides of the small group, but their body language was identical.

I couldn't spend any more time or energy observing them, though, because the forensics officers arrived and called me forward to take my statement. I told them everything.

Pausing after I described the loud sound I'd heard in the prop room, I added, "It almost sounded like there was someone up on the catwalk when I arrived."

There. Now they knew. I could let them handle it from here.

The officers glanced in that direction, noting the frayed wires and bent support arms that hung where the stage light used to.

"We'll look into it," one officer told me, jotting down a note before closing his notebook.

Nodding numbly, I turned away at their dismissal. Carter had moved back a few rows to join the huddle of cast members. His cheeks were red, and his eyes kept flashing about the space as if searching for someone he might yell at.

That person arrived a few moments later. Winnie Wisteria rushed into the theatre, her hair plastered to her face, proving both that the rain had started up again and that she'd hurried to get here, not even stopping to grab a jacket or umbrella. The long, flowing scarves she always wore clung to her in all the wrong places, and her mouth fell open as she noticed Francine's body.

Before she was able to say anything, however, Carter stalked over to her. "This is your fault. The lights are your area, Winnie. You're supposed to check them to make sure accidents like this don't happen."

Winnie's eyes flashed over to the group, but then her attention was back on Carter. "I know. I'm sorry. I ... They were good the last time I checked them."

Surveying the cast members present, I couldn't figure out who Winnie had been looking at. No one so much as flinched or shifted their weight, as if they were all frozen, watching the confrontation between Winnie and Carter.

"Well, it doesn't matter, because you're fired." Carter's whole scalp was a mottled red now; the anger seemed to undulate off him.

Someone coughed. Others whispered. Carter swung around, scowling at the group as if he were daring them to say anything.

But Winnie simply lifted her chin. "You can't fire me. Only Petra can do that."

"I can refuse to work with you on this production, and the next one after that … if I come back." He muttered the last part.

Winnie's eyes turned steely. "And I can argue my case with Petra."

He exhaled a wry laugh. "You really think you have any chance of Petra siding with you after what you pulled last week?" When Winnie blanched in surprise, Carter added, "That's right. I know all about it. And I know I'm doing her a favor by getting rid of you."

The fear and resignation that flashed through my neighbor's features made my stomach flip with unease. What was Carter alluding to with that comment? What did Winnie pull with Petra? Whatever it was, it sounded big enough that it could give Petra a motive to send Winnie the truffles of trouble Julian had intercepted.

Without another word, Winnie whirled back the way she'd come and raced out of the theatre. I couldn't tell if it was rain or tears clinging to her cheeks.

"Meg." Ripley waved me over to where she'd appeared in the back row of the auditorium.

Pretending to get a call, I pulled out my phone and held it up to my ear. "Hey," I whispered once I'd reached where Ripley stood. "Find anything?" I was fairly sure the crew and cast couldn't hear me, but I kept an eye on the group just in case. No one even looked in my direction.

Ripley blew a raspberry. "None of them noticed a thing. Janet keeps saying the same thing. Katherine only shook her head, but Nathanial told me the stage isn't his *area*, and he can only see what happens in here if the doors are open, which they weren't when this happened to Francine."

"Not his area?" I whispered.

"Yes, the three of them divided up the place," Ripley explained. "Though, I couldn't get a reason why they would do so out of Nathanial. Janet's area is the stage and auditorium, but she only arrived on the scene moments before us."

My lips twisted into a frown. Strange. The ghosts at the Morrisey had their favorite spots to hang out, but they didn't dictate where the others could or could not go. I mean, Rooftop Rachel never moved, but she also didn't keep other ghosts from joining her on the roof—also maybe because that would entail talking, which she strictly did not do. And the basement ghosts didn't necessarily keep others out, though Ripley and I had steered clear of them for a long time because of their propensity to scare people and spirits alike.

"I told the officers about the sound on the catwalk, and they said they would look into it. Without having heard the sound Janet did, I can't give them more detail." I sighed.

"What happened with Carter and Winnie?" Ripley asked. "I only caught the end of it."

"Oh, he fired her." I widened my eyes to convey how intense the experience had been. "Said it was her job to check the lights."

Suddenly, the chatter in the room ceased. Everyone present in the cast and crew turned toward the house doors. Carter broke off from the group and went to intercept a woman who stormed into the auditorium moments later.

She had to be at least twice my age, maybe more. At first glance, she was the type of person I'd encountered often during my time in the art scene in New York City and Chicago. Her button-up blouse was a rose-gold silk, topped with a Macintosh jacket that had to be worth at least three of my paintings. Her thick-rimmed black glasses offset the smooth skin of her face, proving she either got regular facials or had been using expensive skincare products her whole life. The woman was rich, and I'd bet anything she was the mysterious Petra we'd heard about.

"Ooh, the owner?" Ripley asked, craning her neck as she echoed my exact thoughts.

"Yes, and based on something Carter said, I think she could be the one who sent those chocolates to Winnie."

Eleven

Ripley's gaze held on to me tightly in lieu of reaching out and grabbing my arm. "Tell me everything."

I glanced around. I didn't want to talk here, and it wasn't the best time. This was the first time I'd seen Petra. I wanted to talk to her if I could.

"It looks like you're not going to get a chance to talk to Petra anytime soon," Ripley said, reading the intentions behind my hesitation.

She was right. The police had called over the owner of the theatre, and a disgruntled lineup of cast members behind her made it clear she was going to be answering questions for a while.

Running my tongue over my teeth as I thought, I gestured for Ripley to follow me out into the lobby. With everyone crowded around the stage, and the police checking the catwalk, it would be the only area where we wouldn't be overheard.

I slipped into the women's restroom and moved to the far corner, keeping my phone in my hand. If someone walked in, it would just look like I was on my phone ... in the bathroom. Not my best plan, but the bathroom door made such an awful creaking sound, I would know right away if anyone else entered.

I faced Ripley once the door was closed. "When Carter fired Winnie, he hinted at something big having gone down between Winnie and Petra last week. Winnie told him that only Petra could fire her, but when she threatened to get the owner involved, Carter said something along the lines of *there's no way she'll help you after what you did to her last week*." I widened my eyes.

"What could the person who runs the lighting booth have done to the owner of the theatre?" Ripley frowned.

"I don't know, but based on how everyone reacted when she got here, I'm guessing Petra doesn't have many fans among the cast and crew."

"That's not entirely true." A man's voice echoed through the restroom.

Ripley let out a quick yelp and my body jerked in surprise.

My heart hammered as I scanned the small space. The door hadn't opened, I could see into all three stalls from where I stood, and there wasn't anyone but us in the—

"Nathanial?" Ripley asked, warning ringing in her tone. Her question was met with silence. "Am I going to have to take back what I told Meg earlier about you *not* being a creepy bathroom peeper? I vouched for you, man."

There was a beat of silence. "I'm technically standing in the entryway into the bathroom. I can't see anything."

Sighing, Ripley rolled her eyes. "Get in here."

A moment later, the transparent spirit I'd seen wandering around the lobby stepped forward, eyes downcast. His gaze met mine, but then he immediately looked back at his shoes. "Hello, Megan. It's nice to meet you."

I wasn't sure if I could return the compliment. I didn't think meeting anyone in a public restroom was a nice way to be introduced.

"What did you mean when you said Meg was wrong about people not trusting Petra?" Ripley placed a hand on her hip.

"A lot of them don't. They think she's stuck up and more worried about her image with her rich, charity-running friends than this theatre. But there are a few here who are loyal to her. Damien, for example, owes her his life," Nathanial explained. "She took that boy in when he had no one else, and she lets him live here."

"Wait." I frowned. "Damien *lives* here?"

Nathanial confirmed, saying, "That 'storage space' behind the ticket booth? That's his apartment. Even goes up to the second floor. He's lived here for years."

Carter's tour yesterday had been so quick, I hadn't been able to note anything too suspicious. But now that I thought about it, the dismissive way he flicked his fingers toward the door and said it was just storage made me wonder if even he was aware Damien lived on the premises.

"Petra's his foster mom?" Ripley asked, her voice tight with emotion.

"Sure. You could call her that." Nathanial apathetically raised his shoulder, obviously not understanding the significance of that title to Ripley like I did. But now wasn't the time to get into my ghostly friend's childhood in the foster system, especially judging by Ripley's tensed posture.

"Do you know anything about what happened between Winnie and Petra?" I asked, moving us on to a different topic.

Nathanial squinted one eye. "No, but he was on the phone with Petra the other day, and he mentioned that he thought Winnie needed to go. I only heard his side of the beginning of the conversation because he was walking through the lobby and went out of my area before I could hear much more than that."

"He said Winnie needed to go?" Ripley asked no one in particular. "And then he fires her now. That's interesting."

"Would be a little more interesting if we had the rest of the conversation," I muttered under my breath.

Ripley eyed me and then fixed Nathanial with a look that said *she's not wrong*.

His back straightened, giving his spirit a rigid quality. "Talk to Katherine or Janet about that."

"That's the thing. Janet doesn't seem to notice anything that happens around here, even when it's a person getting crushed by a light in the middle of the stage she spends so much time on, and Katherine won't talk to either of us." Frustration rose inside me. "Why can't you go in other parts of the theatre, again?"

He wouldn't meet my eyes as he said, "It's a long story,

but it's for the better if we don't. We don't exactly … get along."

Fingers curling into fists, I let the motion release the worst of my annoyance. This was too important for us to be held back by the whims of ghosts.

"Nathanial, a woman has died. Someone else is in a coma because of what's going on in this theatre. If there was ever a time for the three of you to suck it up and be civil for two minutes, it would be now."

Ripley clapped at the end of my speech.

Nathanial let his eyebrows rise in defiance, but he didn't argue. "Fine. It's your funeral."

I swallowed, hoping he wasn't speaking literally as we left the restroom and went in search of the other ghosts.

❦

THE MOMENT we stepped into the prop room, Katherine was there, tapping her ghostly foot.

"Oh, no. You can't bring him back here." She wagged a finger in our faces.

"So, she *can* speak," Ripley teased.

Katherine sent her a simpering sneer that made me think she'd probably been a rather good actress back when she was alive, especially if the part called for looking utterly livid with someone.

"We know you have rules, and this isn't usually allowed, but this is officially an emergency," I whispered, looking past —through—her, around the space, to make sure there weren't any police officers or cast members lingering back here.

Katherine nodded toward the stage. "Fine, but you get to go fetch *Blondie*. I'm not spending a single second more than I have to with that idiot."

My mouth parted in surprise. Ripley puffed out her cheeks.

"Harsh," Rip whispered. "I'll go get her since you'll be noticed, Megs."

With that, my best friend disappeared, leaving me to stand awkwardly in between the two remaining ghosts. I could feel their hatred for one another emanating from them in wisps of ghostly energy.

"So … how long have you known each other?" I asked with a cringe, willing Ripley to hurry.

Katherine sniffed in disgust, and Nathanial muttered something that sounded like "It feels like forever" as he wandered away. But before the ghostly director could get more than a few yards from us, Ripley appeared again.

Alone.

She glanced behind her and did a double take when she found the space empty. Sighing, she disappeared again, reappearing moments later with the blonde ghost I'd seen hanging out on the stage earlier.

"Janet, this is Meg. Meg, Janet." Ripley's patience must've been paper thin at that point.

I held up a hand in greeting. "Nice to meet you, officially, Janet."

She smiled sweetly, but her attention caught on the painting I'd finished earlier. "Oh, that's beautiful."

Her reaction brought to mind Imogen's appreciation for my art earlier. Their similar hair color made me soften, wondering if she was going to be kind as I'd found Imogen to be once she was removed from the rest of the cast.

"Shame it has to be kept in here with the ugliest person I know." Janet adopted a sneer before she added, "Personality-wise, of course. Wouldn't want to insult the only thing Katherine cares about: her looks."

There went *that* hope. I stuffed the thought that things might look up and resolved to get through the information I needed from them as quickly as possible so we could end this get-together.

"Look, you three." I fixed them with my best impression of Nancy when she was in her *stern* mode. "Winnie is my neighbor, and someone tried to poison her a few days ago. They poisoned a different person in our building instead, so I could really use your help if I have any hope of stopping whoever is trying to kill her." I hoped that statement would sober them up a bit. "I need to know if anyone has information about what Winnie and Petra fought about last week. Or, if you know of anyone here who might want to hurt Winnie."

Katherine stepped forward. "Well, if you ask me—"

"Of course, the ice queen speaks first," Janet deadpanned. "Everyone shut up so we can hear what Katherine the Great has to say about the situation when she wasn't even in that part of the theatre when it happened."

"Don't. Call. Me. That." Katherine's jaw was so tense, I worried she might break teeth, until I remembered she didn't have teeth anymore.

Janet put on an innocent expression and blinked from Katherine to Nathanial. "I'm sorry, that *is* what you wanted people to call you, isn't it?" Janet tapped a ghostly finger against her lip. "I mean, you could deny it, if I hadn't found the piece of paper you'd signed with the nickname, practicing signatures for your fans." Janet broke into a fit of laughter, clutching at her stomach as she bent over.

Nathanial bared his teeth at us in an apology, though I noticed he did nothing to stop the fight.

Katherine snapped back with, "At least I *had* fans. I never had to pay people to come to opening night and bring me flowers so it seemed like I had a lineup of admirers." The look Katherine fixed Janet with—something that was simultaneously looking down her nose while also sizing her up—sent goosebumps tingling across my skin.

"Ladies, ladies." Nathanial stepped forward, holding his hands out like he might if he were stepping into a ring with trained lions he wanted to hold back. "Listen, we can be civil for a few minutes? Surely."

Janet made a gagging sound. "Stop calling us *ladies*, Nathanial." His name sounded like poison on her lips. "The way you drag it out sounds super creepy."

"Yes, please spare us your *male opinion* on why we're being too emotional." Katherine glowered in disgust.

"At least you can't put your paws all over us anymore." Janet shook out her spirit as if she'd gotten the willies. "That's my favorite part of being dead."

"Tell me about it. The number of times he touched me on the back or put a hand on my waist..." Katherine didn't finish that sentence.

Nathanial, who'd seemed rather docile—kind even—up until that point, fumed with anger. His eyes narrowed into slits as he regarded the other ghosts. "I'm sorry for caring about my actors. I can't help it if I'm a touchy-feely person."

Even Ripley and I shared a disgusted glance at that line.

"Can we please focus?" Ripley clapped three times. "A man is in a coma, and Winnie might be about to join him if we can't figure out who sent her those chocolates."

"Winnie? The annoying one who works the lights?" Katherine cocked a hip. "Ask Nathanial about her. He probably *cares* so much about her."

Janet, it seemed, quickly hopped off the making-fun-of-Nathanial train the moment she saw an opening to make fun of Katherine again. "At least he cares for somebody. The only way I think you'd show any sort of human emotion would be to hold up a mirror in front of you."

Ripley opened her hands and let them fall back to her sides as she looked to me for help. Feelings of absolute frustration and anger warred inside of me. Did I always have to be the one to fix everything? She was a ghost, and so were these guys. She should handle this instead of always turning to me for help.

I almost opened my mouth to vent these feelings at her before I put my attitude in check. Why was I getting mad at Ripley, of all souls? Clearly, I was tired from a very long day, bent out of sorts by finding Francine dead, and then having to stand here listening to these three fight. I obviously didn't have the patience to deal with petty ghosts today.

Shaking my head, I said, "Fine. I can see why you stay

separated. Lesson learned." I backed toward the door. "We shouldn't have asked."

Ripley followed me. The three bickering ghosts didn't even notice as we left.

Twelve

Ripley and I walked by the stage on our way out, but everyone had cleared out except for a few officers. It looked like I wasn't going to get a chance to talk to Petra today. It was probably for the better. Fatigue felt like a second heavy winter coat, dragging me down as I walked through the theatre lobby. The sun was already setting by the time we stepped out onto the street.

"At least it's not raining anymore," Ripley said, obviously sharing in my disappointment that it was already growing dark.

I yawned. "True."

"So?" she asked. "Where do we go from here?"

"Well, the ghosts may not have been *much* help, but Nathanial gave us at least one lead: Damien." I must've been tired because I didn't even try to hide the fact that I was talking to thin air, as far as everyone else walking along the streets of Seattle was concerned. "Petra and Winnie obviously got in a fight. Depending on what it was about and how serious the situation was, Petra could very well have sent those chocolates to Winnie because of whatever happened. But she's not the only one anymore. If Damien is Petra's foster son, and he lives at the theatre, he might've tried to hurt Winnie on behalf of Petra."

"Damien will be harder to get information out of than most people. He barely speaks."

"Also true," I said, dread building in my stomach. "It'd be nice if Winnie would help at all, but she's told me even less than the ghosts have."

A man passing by on the street glanced reproachfully in my direction, not only because I was talking to myself, but because I'd used the word ghosts. I stayed quiet for the rest of our trip back to the Morrisey.

My body sagged more with each step, feeling like it was ten o'clock at night instead of barely dinnertime. With how early it became dark during this time of year, it sure felt like it was time for bed.

The Morrisey lobby looked like a beacon, lit up like it was in the darkness.

Ripley let her head fall back in bliss. "Ah, it feels so good to be home. At least it feels like people are happy to see us here—unlike some places."

"Tell me about it," I whispered as I pushed through the front doors.

Loving the Morrisey was in my bones. It was never a surprise how stepping foot through the front doors put a smile on my face, putting me instantly at ease. That feeling was amplified today. After spending time at the Third Avenue Theatre for two days in a row, I was starting to realize that showbiz might not be for me. The atmosphere was tense, and an air of competition and anxiety clung to every surface, like paint under fingernails that just won't come out.

Pushing through the front doors once I'd used my key, I turned right to see two of my fifth-floor neighbors were hanging out in the lobby with the Conversationalists. Iris and Alyssa were seated across from Art and Darius. Opal was snuggled into the armchair closest to the fireplace, working on a new book of puzzles.

"Nutmeg!" Darius said so boisterously that Alyssa jumped. "How was your day at the theatre?"

Opal set down her book. "Yeah, learn anything good?"

Pulling a breath in through my nose, I said, "I'm working on it, but they're a bunch of closed books up there." I left it at that, not wanting to explain everything that had happened today with Francine. Winnie probably wouldn't want the whole building to know she'd been fired either.

The fact that I was being my own sort of closed book in keeping all of that to myself was not lost on me—glass houses and all.

I turned my attention to Iris and Alyssa. A canvas tote bag sat next to Iris, likely full of books she'd brought back and forth between her job at the Seattle Public Library and home. No doubt she'd been here chatting since she came home for the evening, not even making it upstairs yet. Alyssa, however, was wearing fuzzy slippers and a sweatshirt, so she must've been up to her apartment already and had come down to talk. Alyssa's sweatshirt, though casual, still looked like it cost more than most of my clothes, a brand logo at her hip confirming that the piece was one of the fancy designers she bought from in her position at Nordstrom's.

As if she could see the questions lining up in my mind, Alyssa said, "We're hiding out down here because Taylor's boyfriend is over, and he's playing the most awful music." She scrunched up her nose.

Iris blew out a thin breath. "It's a good thing Edna can barely hear anymore. I kind of wish I had a hearing aid I could turn off."

"Ah, I've encountered the boyfriend too." I grimaced. "He's ... interesting."

But Alyssa was already shaking her head. "I can tell you *for sure* that he is not. I accidentally rode the elevator with him yesterday and he talked the whole time about crypto." She said the last word in a bad imitation of the guy's voice.

Next to me, Ripley snorted out a laugh.

"I'm surprised he spoke to you," Opal said. "Every time I see either him or Taylor, they've always got things in or on their ears." She mimed headphones.

Art nodded seriously. "It's because they're always making or watching TicTacs."

Now it was my turn to chuckle. "TikToks," I corrected him.

Darius touched his finger to his nose.

Oh, boy. I loved these people. But I'd be lying if I said the exhaustion of the day wasn't getting to me, so I said goodbye and turned toward the mailboxes. A bright-pink note had been slipped in with the rest of my mail.

You've got mail! Actually, it's a package. Go see Nancy for your prize (package).

Biting back a smile, I glanced over at Ripley, who was reading the note over my shoulder.

"Nance is really going all out to try to make this package thing fun for everyone, isn't she?" Ripley huffed out a laugh.

Anticipation bolstered my mood as I locked my mailbox and went to Nancy's apartment across the hallway. She answered moments after I pressed her buzzer, wearing her reading glasses and carrying an open book, as if it was so good, she might continue reading while we had our conversation.

But when she saw that it was me, Nancy said, "Oh, good. Nutmeg, you're just the person I wanted to talk to." She jogged over to the nearest table so she could set down the book.

Lifting my eyebrows in question, I held up the pink paper from my mailbox. "Because I have a package?"

Nancy shook her head but quickly followed with a nod. "No, but we can get that at the same time. I wanted to ask you a favor."

"Sure," I said as I followed her across the hallway to the mechanical room where the access door for the mailroom was located. "What's up?"

Unlocking the door to the mechanical room and ushering me inside, Nancy waited until the door was shut behind her before whispering, "I just wanted to know what happened at the theatre today, but I don't want to be a *gossip.*" She emphasized the last word as if it were akin to growing a second head. "Winnie came storming in about an hour ago telling me she wouldn't be making it to Thanksgiving dinner because she got fired."

The statement shocked me. That Winnie even shared so much with Nancy spoke to how out of sorts she must've been upon returning to the Morrisey that evening. I wanted to look at Ripley to see her reaction to that piece of news, but Nancy was watching me too closely and would surely notice.

"She told you she was fired?"

Nancy tipped her head from side to side. "Well, she may have said it was your fault she wouldn't ever be going back to that theatre, but yeah, in so many words."

"*My* fault?" Incredulity filled my question.

"I'm sure she's just shocked, dear." Nancy patted my hand.

"Sure. What happened today was pretty shocking."

Nancy's eyes went wide as I told her about Francine's death and how the director blamed Winnie.

"Oh, no wonder she doesn't think she'll feel up to being around anyone on Thursday." Nancy placed a hand over her heart. "Being accused of something like that."

Sympathy filled the places in my heart that had so recently been crammed with frustration toward my neighbor, and I had to agree with Nance.

"Oh!" Nancy exclaimed, almost making me jump. "I forgot that I was going to ask if you wouldn't mind bringing cranberry sauce tomorrow. Would you?" Nancy asked sheepishly. "It was what Winnie was supposed to bring, and if I can't count on her coming…" She left the sentence hanging.

"Art and Darius will never stop talking about it if we don't have any," I finished for her, knowing all too well what the consequences would be.

Luckily, the guys preferred the jellied canned stuff, so I

wouldn't have to add any more cooking to my list. Grabbing a couple of cans at the store would do the trick.

"Yep." I bobbed my head. "I can do that."

"You're a lifesaver, dear. Now, let's get you that package." Nancy turned to the mailroom and unlocked that door as well.

On the other side of the wall of open mailboxes to our right, there was a long shelf that ran the length of the room. Packages were stacked there, each with a different colored paper slip taped to the side. She found one with a pink piece of paper and grabbed the note from my hand, putting the matching slips of pink paper back in a stack at the end of the shelf. The blue, green, purple, and orange packages must've belonged to the residents with the corresponding colored notes from Nancy in their mail cubbies. Leave it to Nance to find an organized way to distribute the packages.

"A little system I came up with to make this whole searching gig faster." She twiddled her fingers in the air.

"Thank you." I held up the package, pretty sure it was the new set of paints I'd ordered last week. "I'll see you around."

Blowing me a kiss as she locked up, us parting ways in the lobby, Nancy said, "See you Thursday."

"Winnie must really be in a bad place if she's not coming to Thanksgiving," Ripley whispered once we were alone in the stairwell.

The woman had loudly proclaimed it to be her favorite holiday each year, especially when she didn't have to cook, hence her contribution being cans of sauce she merely had to open.

"I think we should pay her a visit to make sure she's doing okay."

Ripley agreed, and we stopped at the fourth floor instead of going all the way up to the fifth. Tucking my package and mail under my left arm, I pressed Winnie's buzzer.

Winnie opened the door, her wispy scarves whooshing around her with the movement. The moment she recognized me, her features hardened even more. "Oh, it's you."

"What a warm greeting," Ripley said, sarcasm dripping from her tone.

I ignored them both. "I came to check on you, Winnie."

She blew out a raspberry and swatted the air between us with a manicured hand. "Oh, because of Carter firing me? It's fine."

"Didn't seem fine earlier," Ripley said out of the corner of her mouth.

"You seemed really upset at the theatre." I took a slightly more tactful angle than my ghostly best friend. I didn't mention what Nancy had told me about how Winnie had blamed me, not wanting to throw the manager under the bus like that.

"I was just surprised. That's all. I'm actually glad to get out of that place. It's cursed anyway, and I'm sure it's going to close within the year because of it." Winnie hung on to the door, pulling it closer as if she didn't want me to see inside.

That wasn't unusual. She'd always been secretive. Even though most other residents would've invited me in by now, I had never gotten such an offer from Winnie. If I could just get my foot over her threshold, Ripley might be able to go inside. But because my ghostly friend couldn't snoop around, I was going to have to stick to asking questions.

"Winnie," I began, choosing my words carefully, "what did you and Petra fight about last week? What did Carter mean when he said he knew what happened between you two?"

A flush swept across Winnie's face. "Th-that's none of your business."

"It is if it's a motive for Petra to have sent you those chocolates," I countered. "Come on. You said I could help you figure out who sent them. In order to do that, you have to open up to me."

Winnie backed away, as if she would close the door in my face. "I have to do no such thing. What happened between me and Petra was nothing. It's not your concern." She pushed the door toward me.

"Wait," I said, causing her to pause. A defeated breath leaked past my teeth. "Okay. Well, I'm going to take care of the cranberry sauce for Art and Darius, so if you still want to come to Thanksgiving, you don't have to bring anything but yourself. We'd love to see you."

Winnie's indifferent mask, the one that reminded me so much of Katherine, slipped a little, and the woman nodded. "I'll think about it." Then she shut the door.

Thirteen

I had just flopped onto the couch, snuggling my face into Anise's soft fur, when there was a knock on my door. Three barks rang out from the hallway, followed by a deep voice, saying, "You don't need to do that at other people's doors, Leo. Warning barks are just for ours." The dog let out three more barks at the verbal cue, and Laurie groaned.

Immediately, the weight of the day drifted away, replaced by excitement. Grinning like a fool, I raced over to the door, opening it and sinking to the floor in one swift movement. Leo rushed forward as far as his leash would allow, which was right into my arms. He licked at my face and wiggled in front of me happily for a few moments before I planted a kiss on his nose and stood to greet Laurie.

"Hey," I said, not overthinking it when I wrapped my arms around him.

Apparently, Laurie was all about my impulsivity because he pulled me even closer, leaning down to kiss me. A faint squeak of happiness came from the couch, but I could tell Ripley was trying to keep herself under control. Still, it made me smile into the kiss as he deepened it.

"What?" he asked as he pulled back and matched my grin.

I pressed my lips together, finding it hard to erase the happiness displayed there. "I just like doing that."

His lips tugged to one side. "Good. Me too." He leaned forward and kissed me again.

A small whine came from the doorway, and we broke apart long enough to turn our attention to Leo, who was sitting very patiently, waiting for us to be done with our greeting.

"Dude, cool it." Laurie cocked an eyebrow at his dog. "If you get to slobber all over her when you see her, so can I."

A laugh bubbled out of me, and I closed the door. As I turned around, I noticed Laurie held a cloth grocery bag in the same hand that clutched Leo's leash.

"What's that?" I pointed.

His eyes lit up. "Have you had dinner yet?"

Suddenly, the bag looked familiar. And then there were the rich, spicy scents wafting from it. I sucked in a breath. "You did *not* bring me some of Lynae's food." I made grabby hands toward the bag.

"It's times like this that I really wish I could smell," Ripley said dreamily as she wafted closer.

"She and Dad say hi, by the way." Laurie called behind him as he walked Leo over to the couch so he could meet Anise.

Leo, of course, was a complete gentleman, and merely

wagged his tail as he sniffed the kitten and let her check him out. Once she rubbed her head against his, Laurie nodded and let Leo off his leash, warning the dog to give the kitten space. He did, opting to follow Laurie back toward me and the kitchen instead of bothering her anymore.

"I only worked a half day today, so I went to Mom and Dad's for lunch," he told me now that we could relax around the pets. "Which, as you can tell, lasted until almost dinner, so that's all yours. But you know Mom; she never lets anyone leave her house without a bag of food." He swiped his palm across his forehead. "I didn't tell them about us just yet."

I halted my greedy piling of food onto a plate. Ripley turned her attention to Laurie as well.

"Is there a reason you didn't?" I asked. Was he having doubts about us?

The lines of his throat tightened. "Honestly? Because I think they'll *insist* you come to Thanksgiving with us if they know."

Relaxing now that I knew his reasoning wasn't something to worry about, I went back to dishing up the food.

"I wouldn't put it past Mom to call Nancy and tell her that you had to come to ours instead of the Morrisey gathering." He shook his body in a shiver as if his mother's resourcefulness scared him.

"I can stop by after we finish up here on Thursday, if you want." I glanced sidelong at him as I popped the loaded plate in the microwave. "You know the Morrisey dinner is more of a lunch anyway."

Laurie exhaled a laugh through his nose. "That's right. I forgot they eat at two."

While the Conversationalists were notorious night owls, the rest of the older population in the building, including Nancy, preferred a much earlier schedule and didn't want to "eat too close to bedtime."

"We could tell my parents then," Laurie said.

I grabbed a fork. "Sounds like a plan."

Ripley let out a quiet "Bleh." Then said, "The pair of you are way too cute. I'm going to hang out at Zoe's place where it's quiet." She winked as she floated past me, disappearing through the wall.

Once my food was ready, I slid onto one of the stools at the bar separating my small kitchen from the rest of the space. With a studio apartment, there wasn't necessarily room for a table, especially if I wanted a desk for my painting supplies.

Instead of taking a seat on the stool next to me, Laurie moved into the kitchen and poured himself a glass of water. He leaned on the counter, facing me. "So, how was your day?"

"Much less pleasant than yours." I took a bite of food, savoring the amazing flavor before swallowing, and adding, "Someone died at the theatre today. A stage light fell on her."

It took longer to get through the story than it should've because I was too hungry to abstain from eating until I was done speaking. Laurie was patient through all of the times my story was interrupted by me stopping to shovel another bite of food in my mouth, chewing, and swallowing. I could tell his mind was working by the way his jaw clenched every time I mentioned another odd happening in the aftermath of Francine's death.

"Do stage lights often fall out of nowhere?" he asked.

Raising and lowering a shoulder, I swallowed. "It's the first theatre I've worked at. But the director did fire Winnie, blaming her for incompetence, and the police are investigating."

Laurie paced through my kitchen as he digested the news. His long legs made it so he could only take a step or two before he had to turn around. Leo lifted his head from where he was lying at the foot of my barstool, wondering what was bothering his favorite human.

"Any leads in the Winnie case?"

"A couple, actually. I learned that Winnie and the owner of the theatre, Petra, got in some kind of altercation last week. I also found out that Damien was raised by Petra, so he could've tried to take Winnie out if he felt the only family he's ever had was threatened."

Laurie ran his tongue between his lips. "Who'd you find out all that from? Are the other cast members finally talking?"

Right. I'd complained to him just yesterday about how tight-lipped the cast and crew were.

"Uh, yeah. Just had to find the right people." Lying to him felt awful. "I think they trust me a little more ... now that I've been there for two days," I added, realizing how little sense that made.

But Laurie seemed to buy it. "Good," he said, eyeing my empty plate. "Want me to wash that for you?"

I leaned my elbows on the bar. "You bring me food *and* do the dishes? You're the dreamiest."

He chuckled, taking my plate, and turning on the water.

"I'm not sure what you have planned tonight, but there's a new Teenage Mutant Ninja Turtles movie out." His eyes glittered with excitement. "I thought we could watch it."

"What? Yes, yes. A thousand times yes." Jumping off my stool, I startled Leo, who got to his feet and jogged with me as I raced over to turn on the television.

Ten minutes later, all four of us were cuddled on the couch. Anise was in my lap, and Leo had curled up on my legs to my left. To my right? I snuggled against Laurie, who had his arm resting on the back of the couch, wrapped around my shoulders.

It felt so incredibly natural. I wondered if some of the ease was a direct result of the sheer amount of time I'd spent picturing what it would be like to be with Laurie. Or, maybe, it was like this for every couple who started out as good friends. Either way, I couldn't have asked for a better night.

Well, all except the fact that I'd lied to him earlier when he'd asked about who'd given me the info on Petra and Damien. Just like this relationship, the lie had come so effortlessly. But I didn't have to wonder about what had caused that ease. I'd spent most of my life hiding my ability to see ghosts, it was second nature now.

If Laurie and I were really going to make this work, though, I needed to be honest with him. Right?

My heart reminded me that even Penny, the aunt who'd raised me, didn't know about my gift. Penny was different, though. I loved my aunt more than anything, but the woman wasn't the most observant. She always made me feel wanted and loved, but she'd never wanted to be a mother, and I think she lacked some of those shrewd instinctual mother skills.

Lynae, for instance, could tell if teenage Laurie had been lying with a single glance. And she'd raised an equally attentive son. He watched, listened, paid attention. It had been fine when we were kids, playing together around the building. But if we were going to make a real relationship work, I didn't know if I could continue to lie.

Regardless of the movie having us rolling with laughter and happily nostalgic, the question about whether to tell Laurie remained after he left for the evening.

"Oh, no." Ripley tutted the moment she returned to the apartment, obviously having heard Laurie leave. "You just had the man of your dreams all to yourself for the evening. There's no room for sour faces tonight." She wagged her index finger in my face.

"There is when you're lying to the man of your dreams." I pouted, then filled her in on how easily the lies had come to me when we were discussing Winnie's potential poisoner.

"Then don't." Ripley shrugged.

"What? Like, tell Laurie I see ghosts? That I've been able to my entire life? Just like that?"

"Yes, Meg. He's Laurie. If anyone will understand, it's him."

Her words gave me pause, not because I disagreed with her, but because it was opposite of any advice she'd ever given me on the topic.

"You've always said that if I told people, they'd start treating me differently." I hated that I sounded whiny, but it felt a little like the floor of the apartment was shifting under my feet. "You said that I couldn't trust people to see me through the information, that they'd either try to use me or think I was losing my grip on reality."

She lowered her chin. "I did. But things are different now." Ripley glanced away, toward the window where she'd spent so many nights standing and staring out since losing the love of her afterlife, Clark.

That movement alone told me it wasn't just that things were different between me and Laurie now that we were dating. She meant things were different with us. Ripley was going to move on someday. She wouldn't always be here for me, and she wanted me to have allies—people I could trust with my gift.

Swallowing the panic that threatened to climb up my throat at the reminder, I nodded. "Okay. I'll think about it."

She smiled back at me, then motioned toward the television. "Want to watch trash TV until you have to go to bed?"

My heart warmed. "Of course." I clicked on our favorite reality show. After the intro scene, while the theme song played, I asked her, "Are you doing okay? I know hearing about Damien being in foster care might've brought up some stuff with you, and I wanted to check in."

Ripley looked down at her hands. "I'll admit that it was kind of a punch to the gut."

I reached out, placing my hand next to hers on the couch. Ripley didn't talk much about growing up in the system. She was even sparse on the details about the couple she'd stayed with the longest, the ones she'd considered her only family until me. All I really knew was that they'd moved away after she'd died. I'd asked throughout the years, but my questions were always met with Winnie-style ambiguity or avoidance.

"Well, I'm here if you want to talk about it."

"I know you are." She patted my hand with hers, the chill of her spirit passing through my body not bothering me in the least, just as her avoidance didn't concern me.

Ripley was my family, and I'd wait until she was ready to talk.

Fourteen

The next morning, Damien was behind the ticket counter when Ripley and I arrived at the theatre. We'd come early, since I wanted to leave around lunchtime to get my shopping done for Thanksgiving.

"Well, well, well." Ripley rubbed her hands together, showing me that she thought we should jump at the chance to question Damien right away.

I couldn't argue, especially since we were alone in the lobby. Veering to the left, I hiked my bag higher on my shoulder. I'd brought in a few of my own supplies today, knowing I would need different tools to create the effects I wanted for the second flat.

Damien didn't even look up when I stopped in front of the ticket booth. Based on the list sitting on the counter and the candy in piles all around it, he was doing an inventory of the concessions now that Francine was gone.

"Say something," Ripley whispered, hunching her body in discomfort at the growing silence.

"Are you taking over the ticket booth?" I asked, leaving off the unnecessary addition of *now that Francine is dead*.

Damien grunted. "Maybe."

"A man of many words." Ripley slapped her hand onto her forehead.

I opened my mouth, about to push him with a second question, when...

My vision narrowed to the stack of boxes behind Damien. To be more specific, boxes of chocolate truffles. The very same chocolates someone sent to Winnie on Saturday laced with fentanyl, and the ones responsible for the coma Julian was currently in.

Ripley swore as she noticed my silence and followed my gaze.

"Those aren't for sale," Damien said.

My attention flashed over to him. I hadn't even realized he was looking at me, let alone noticing how much I was gaping at the chocolates.

"What are they for?" My voice wobbled, and I took a steadying breath.

As far as I knew, no one at the theatre was aware of Winnie's scare with the chocolates. So, no one would be alarmed to hear me asking about them. A perk of Winnie's secretive nature. But the way Damien's icy gaze stabbed into me quickly reminded me that the one person who *would* know about the significance of the chocolates was the person who'd sent them. The person who'd tried to kill my neighbor.

"Petra buys them for our donors," Damien finally said. He jotted something else down on his list. "Whenever they show up for a performance, they get one of those." He started counting bags of Red Vines.

I gulped. "Petra buys them?"

"More evidence pointing toward her," Ripley said in a singsong voice that sounded more like a cautionary tale than a joyful tune.

Damien's eyes flashed with warning. "Francine bought them on Petra's orders." He went back to counting the licorice.

Francine. Who was now dead. Who Winnie told me not to bother looking into.

"Winnie would've recognized the chocolates. Don't you think?" Ripley asked.

I tugged on my ear, letting my best friend know that I did. But even if I hadn't been standing in front of Damien, I'm not sure if I would've been able to answer my friend. My voice caught. Because ... what if Winnie had known exactly who'd sent her those chocolates? What if Winnie really *was* responsible for the light falling on Francine?

"You didn't happen to see Francine yesterday before the ... accident?" I decided to use the same word everyone else seemed to latch on to, even if I didn't fully believe that was what had happened. "Do you know why she was on the stage in the first place?"

The muscles in Damien's throat tightened as he swallowed. "Nope." His cold eyes held mine in some kind of eye-contact-based dare.

"Right." I shifted my bag. This wasn't going anywhere. It looked like I was going to have to come to terms with a hard truth: Damien wasn't any more helpful than the ghosts had been. None of the souls who were here the most, who *should* know the most, were going to help us. "Well, I've got work to do."

Without even waiting for a response—because based on the rest of our "conversation," I wouldn't get one—I left for the prop room.

The moment I set down my stuff, however, my phone rang. An odd mixture of excitement and longing collided in my chest, making it hard to breathe as I saw my aunt's name on my phone's display.

"Hey, Penny." I gripped the phone tight to my ear, as if having it close might feel like getting a hug from her.

Ripley beamed at me but floated off into the back part of the prop room to give me space.

"Kiddo! How are you?" Penny's voice was bright, just what I needed to hear to bolster my spirits in this dreary theatre surrounded by liars and most likely a potential killer.

"Oh, you know. I'm fine."

"I actually don't know." She let out a light chuckle. "I'm sorry it's been so long since I called. I had a book due and, well, you know how much of an office troll I become when I'm on deadline."

I giggled, remembering when she used to call herself that when I was a kid. She made up a whole story about the office troll, who survived exclusively on coffee and licorice-flavored jellybeans. Sometimes she wouldn't move from her desk all day, hunched over her keyboard, clacking away, muttering about subplots and character arcs. I would bring her food and make sure she drank water during the worst of the time crunches, when she had to turn around a manuscript extra fast.

"No worries, Penny," I assured her. "I've been busy too."

"Oh? That sounds promising." I could picture my aunt settling on her couch with a mug of tea and at least five dogs piled around her. "Your paintings still selling well at the speakeasy?"

"They are, but I'm also doing something else on the side."

I hesitated for a moment, wondering if I should tell her about the attempt on Winnie's life or how Julian was in a coma. She still messaged with the Morrisey folks regularly, so it probably wouldn't be long until she found out, but I decided I didn't particularly want to talk about those things while I was here, and any number of cast or crew members might overhear me admitting to knowing Winnie or searching for whoever wanted her dead.

"I got a job at the Third Avenue Theatre, painting sets for their production of *Singing in the Rain*."

Penny was silent for a beat. Maybe she already knew about Winnie.

"Meg, are you sure you want to work there? Isn't that place, like, cursed or something?"

Winnie had said the same thing last night. My mind latched on to Francine's death and the combative cast. "You know, this is only my third day, but I think you might be right. It's … interesting here." I left it at that, then asked, "Wait, what have you heard?" Maybe Penny knew something about the three frustrating ghosts who haunted the place, or how I might get them to help me.

But she merely said, "It's been on the brink of shutting down for years. Decades, maybe." There was a growling in the background, followed by a bark. "Hey, you two. Knock it off. Sorry, the weather's icky today, so the kids are restless."

Penny always referred to her many dogs as "the kids." I smiled, nostalgia wrapping around my shoulders at my aunt's familiarness.

"Anyway, back to the theatre. I think people mostly said the thing about the curse because it used to be quite popular. It was small compared to the Paramount and the Fifth Avenue, but the shows they used to put on were fabulous. Then, suddenly, they just went downhill." She was silent for a moment, probably shrugging. "Pioneer Square residents can be dramatic, but maybe throw some salt over your shoulder just in case."

Chuckling, I said, "I can do that."

"Okay, well, I just wanted to call and wish you a happy early Thanksgiving. I know you'll probably be busy with the Morrisey dinner tomorrow, so I wanted to talk today."

"Happy Thanksgiving to you, too, Pen. Are you going to celebrate at all?"

While Scotland obviously didn't celebrate American Thanksgiving, they had a lot of other fun holidays Penny was excited to experience firsthand.

"There's another American woman in town. She's coming over, and we're going to do our best to recreate some dishes even though neither of us are particularly good cooks."

That was an understatement, at least where Penny was concerned. My aunt was good at many things, but cooking had never been one of them. I'd mostly taken after her, though Ripley was pretty handy in the kitchen and she'd taught me how to make some of her favorites.

"Good luck. I'll be thinking good thoughts for your meal. Love you."

"Love you, too, kid."

I hung up the call and turned toward the large canvas. I needed to put finishing touches on the first one and start on the blocking for the second so it could dry overnight. But before I could even get out my paints, Ripley appeared by my side. Her eyes were wide with what looked like a secret she did not want to keep.

"What?" I asked, glancing behind to make sure no one had entered the prop room since I had.

"You need to come here." The intensity in her expression only increased as Ripley backed up, leading me wherever it was she'd just been. She hadn't stayed in the prop room while I'd been on the phone, apparently, because she moved toward the hallway.

Placing the paintbrush on the nearest stool, I followed. Ripley led me through the lobby, up to the second floor, and to the door of the women's dressing room.

"What is it?" I whispered, wondering why she wouldn't just tell me what she'd found.

My worry increased as she slipped into the dressing room. Ripley wasn't reckless, especially not when it came to me, so I figured the place must be empty if she was leading me inside.

Before I could move, Ripley's head appeared through the door. "Don't worry. It's too early. No one else is in here."

I entered. It was the first time I'd seen inside either of the dressing rooms. Given that Carter had all but glossed over this part of his fastest tour in history, I hadn't ever seen inside. The large space had been divided into smaller dressing rooms by using what looked like cubical walls and curtains for doors.

The lights were on overhead, but each smaller dressing area was dark. Behind me on the door, call sheets were pinned to the wood. I grabbed one, sticking it in my back pocket after confirming that the first scene wasn't meant to start for an hour yet.

Walking through the curtain second on the right, Ripley disappeared into one of the dressing rooms. The one Ripley chose had a sign pinned to the curtain: Yasmine.

I trusted Ripley not to put me in a bad situation and followed her into Yasmine's dressing area. The small space was packed. A rack of costumes took up the cubical wall to my left, a vanity and chair were set up to the right, and there was even a small love seat for her to sit on if she had time to kill.

Even just thinking it, the word *kill* caused a shiver to crawl over my body.

"Look," Ripley said, the sheer volume of her voice making my skin itch with discomfort even though I knew I was the only one who could hear her. She motioned toward the vanity.

Along with the mirror and a fancy ring light, the vanity was cluttered with makeup. I was about to hiss in frustration at Ripley, letting her know that makeup was definitely not worthy of making me sneak into someone's dressing room, but then I caught what she'd actually been pointing out.

Stuck to the clamshell container of Yasmine's blush was a sticker. It was the very same frog-wearing-cowboy-boots sticker I'd seen on the card that came with the poisoned chocolates meant for Winnie.

Petra may have requested the chocolates, and Francine may have been the one to order them, but anyone in the building could've swiped a box from behind the ticket booth if they knew they were there.

This sticker seemed like a calling card, like a warning to Winnie. And even though the person who'd sent the chocolates hadn't signed their name, that sticker was probably just as good as a signature if Yasmine used it on a lot of her belongings.

Sure enough, moving to the shelves in the corner, I found three more items with stickers on them, including Yasmine's copy of the script. As I flipped through, Ripley let out a strangled sound. I was just about to ask her what she'd found when someone cleared their throat behind me.

I froze. Turning slowly, I found Yasmine standing in the entrance to her dressing area, arms crossed. The look on her face could only be described as murderous.

Fifteen

"What are you doing?" Yasmine's question whipped out, snapping in my face.

I normally would've flinched, would've cowered, and made up some excuse. But anger built inside my chest, feeling like an inferno. Suddenly, all that mattered was confronting this person and finding out if she'd sent Winnie those chocolates.

"Where'd you get this sticker?" I asked, jabbing a thumb at the compact on her vanity.

Taken aback by my odd question, Yasmine blinked and then frowned. "No. You don't get to ask the questions here. What are *you* doing in *my* dressing room?"

Okay, so I was going to have to figure out something, and quick. Gaze moving throughout the small space, I settled on the costumes hanging on a rack along the other wall. "I, uh, forgot the color of the dress you wore during one of the numbers I'm making a flat for, and I didn't want the colors to clash."

Ripley nodded, impressed with my lie. Any good feelings I might've had toward my friend's approval dissipated as I remembered that she was the reason I was in this pickle in the first place.

Yasmine checked the dresses hanging on the other side of the dressing room. "Then why are you pawing through my makeup and asking about stickers?"

My conviction faltered. Did I really want to admit I knew about the poisoned chocolates? If Yasmine was the one who sent them, showing my hand like that might very well land me next on her delivery list.

"Oh, I thought I'd seen a sticker like this somewhere else in the theatre. That's all." I shrugged, my nonchalance completely at odds with the intensity I'd come in with at the beginning of our conversation.

Yasmine walked forward to get a better look at the sticker. "Oh, that? Francine gets them for us so we can mark our scripts and stuff, keep everything separate. Well, I guess Francine *got* them for us." She pouted, acting sad at the mention of her deceased coworker.

If I hadn't seen Yasmine on stage, I might have bought her act. But I'd seen her swoon over Don as if she were in love, and then Ripley had overheard her telling a friend how much she hated him. I knew not everything happening before my eyes was the truth.

"What's your history with Winnie like?" I put my hand on my hip.

Yasmine snorted. "Winnie? The lady that works the lights and sound?" Her tone suggested that she had never thought about Winnie once in her entire life. "Why would I have history with her?"

"Maybe the sticker was from Francine," Ripley said.

I had to agree. Even if Yasmine was acting, I wasn't going to be able to get her to admit any different.

"Well, I'll get out of your way, then." I scooted around her.

And just as I was promising to myself never to come back to Yasmine's dressing room again, I saw something I recognized: the purple folder that had been on Winnie's desk just yesterday.

At least, I thought it was that same folder, but I couldn't quite tell. It was tucked under a few other books and scripts. Glancing once more over my shoulder to make sure Yasmine wasn't following me, I headed back to the first floor.

Ripley and I waited until we got back to the prop room before we talked.

"What caught your eye at the end there?" Ripley asked, having noticed my double take.

Whirling on my best friend, I asked, "What were you thinking?"

Ripley blinked.

"You could've just told me you found the sticker. Why'd you put me in that position?" I flailed my arms in the air, needing a physical release for the adrenaline that had built up during my encounter with Yasmine.

Sneering, Ripley said, "You're fine, aren't you?"

"That's not an apology." I began readying my painting supplies so I had something to do other than glare at Ripley. "You know, this isn't the first out-of-character thing you've done this week either. Ripping on Carter with Nathanial? That kind of mean-girl stuff isn't like you, Ripley."

Her hard features softened. "I'm not sure what I was thinking, honestly—in either case. Just now, it was like I had this giddy voice in my head, whispering, *Meg's gotta see this*, and I didn't even think about how I might be putting you in danger. And with Carter ... I had this clear plan of how I could manipulate Nathanial, and I just went for it. I'm not sure what's been coming over me." She looked so confused that I took pity on her and accepted her apology even though anger still boiled inside my veins at the encounter.

Trying to calm myself down even more, I finally told her about the purple folder, how one just like it had been sitting on Winnie's desk yesterday.

"I would go take a look, but it was under those papers, and I can't move that without knocking it all over." Ripley fidgeted next to me, obviously still feeling badly about putting me in danger.

"Which means I'm going to have to find another time to sneak into Yasmine's dressing room, without getting caught."

While I got to work painting, Ripley studied the call sheet I'd swiped from the door of the dressing room. She pointed at a scene about halfway down the list. "Megs, it looks like this first scene uses a lot of cast members. I think that's when we should go."

It was another attempt to patch things up between us.

Checking what she was saying against the schedule, I agreed. "Gotcha."

I worked until I heard Carter scream for the actors to get their butts on the stage. That was my cue. I tiptoed through the backstage area, upstairs, and then snuck back into the dressing room. Instead of messing around, looking at stickers this time, I went straight for the pile of scripts, books, and the purple folder. But it was gone.

"Did she move it?" Ripley asked.

I frowned, glancing around the space. Maybe Ripley hadn't been the only one to notice me staring at the purple folder earlier. Yasmine might've seen my interest and moved it just in case. But where else could she hide something? This was her only personal space. It had to be here somewhere.

I searched, checking underneath the chair, around the vanity, even in between her costumes just in case she'd gotten the idea to hide it in one of them.

Heels clicked on the floor. Based on the quick rhythm of the footsteps, the person was moving fast. Eyes wide, I glanced up at Ripley.

"Hide," she said as the sound moved in our direction.

The only place that would offer any cover in the space was the rack of costumes hanging in the corner. But there were only a handful of dresses, not enough to conceal me. Then I spotted the space under the vanity. It would have to do. Based on the quickness of the footsteps, Yasmine had forgotten something and was rushing back to retrieve it. She'd be gone soon, and I could continue my search ... as long as she didn't see me underneath the vanity.

Crouching down low, I scooted into the open space, pulling the rolling chair toward me so it would help mask me along with the shadows. I held my breath just as the footsteps slowed, coming to a stop in front of the dressing room.

It wasn't Yasmine who slipped through the curtain, however. It was Imogen.

She didn't even glance toward the vanity, thank goodness. Instead, she raced over to the costumes, making me immensely grateful I hadn't tried to hide there.

Flipping through the rack, Imogen settled on a dress I'd seen Yasmine wear during her first scene in the musical, when Kathy meets Don. Imogen pulled something from her pocket and continued to mess with the dress. The chair obstructed my view, though, and I couldn't see exactly what she was doing.

Ripley floated toward me, frowning. "It's a sewing kit," she said, absolute confusion slowing the statement.

Why would Imogen be sewing Yasmine's costumes? And why was she hiding the fact that she was? As if to prove my point, Imogen glanced toward the doorway at a sound, working faster as she turned back to the dress.

At that moment, my knee jerked to the right, silently protesting being bunched up into this pretzel of a position for so long. It banged into the vanity and, to my horror, the movement jostled a tube of lipstick or maybe mascara, because something went rolling above my head.

Imogen jumped, spinning toward the sound. At first, she must not have seen me, but when she stepped closer, she whispered, "Miss Meg? What are you doing here?" She shoved the dress behind her back.

That nickname. I grunted my way out of my hiding spot and got to my feet. Ripley stood by my side for support. Again, that confrontational side of me won out. And unlike when I'd tried it with Yasmine, this time it might work.

Yasmine had the upper hand when she found me in her dressing room. But I'd technically caught Imogen.

"Actually, I'm more interested in what *you're* doing here." I folded my arms in front of me.

Color rushed to Imogen's face. She looked down at the needle and thread in her hands and fluttered her lips in defeat. "I'm taking in Yas's costumes so she thinks she's putting on weight."

"You can't be serious," I said, disappointment releasing from me in a puff of air from my nostrils.

Ripley ran a judgmental eye up and down the woman. "Shameful."

Imogen's mortified expression morphed into anger. "Oh, don't act like Yasmine's a saint. I'm pretty sure she's the reason Francine is dead."

I froze. "What?"

"She'd do anything to protect her mom, and with Winnie threatening her with blackmail, there's no way she would've stopped until Winnie got fired." Imogen shook her head, as if it were merely a shame and not a woman's life. "Though, I doubt Yasmine's the one who actually dropped that light on Francine. With how much Damien's around the catwalk, I'm sure he did it for her."

Putting my palms up in an effort to slow down the barrage of things that were all news to me, I asked, "Who's Yasmine's mom? And why would Damien kill Francine for Yasmine? Also, blackmail?"

It was all making my head spin. Not the least of which was the fact that I'd been right about Imogen's acting yesterday. She *hadn't* thought the light falling on Francine was an accident after all, which meant that Janet might be right about having heard someone on the catwalk.

Ripley's mouth hung open, proving she was equally caught off guard.

Imogen shot me a look that said *don't you know anything?* "Petra is Yasmine's mom."

"But they don't have the same last name." Even as I said it, my reasoning sounded flat. A lot of family members didn't have the same last name.

"They changed it once Yas was old enough so she could continue to work for Petra and no one would know that she was giving her daughter special treatment, bribing directors to give her the best parts." Imogen lifted the costume she held a few inches as if it were proof that she was the lead. "I found out, though. Let's just say, I'm good at finding out things people don't want anyone to know, and it's served me well." A haughty expression overtook Imogen's features.

"And you think Damien would protect Yasmine since she's Petra's daughter?" I asked.

Imogen scoffed. "More like, Damien would protect Yasmine because he's been in love with her for at least a decade. He'd do anything for her."

"Anything?" I gulped.

Imogen cocked her hip. "Any. Thing." She punctuated each word, then moved as if she were going to leave.

"Wait. You said something about blackmail." My words reached out to stop her.

The self-satisfied look she sported narrowed on me. "Why should I tell you? What are you going to give me?"

"Give you?" I gulped.

She crossed her arms. "Carter gives me first pick at the parts for keeping him informed about all the gossip I hear going around the theatre."

"What a piece of work," Ripley said under her breath.

I pushed back my shoulders. "How about you tell me what I want to know, or I'll go tell Yasmine exactly what I found you doing in here. I'd bet if word got out, your reputation for being a champion of women in the industry wouldn't hold up so well."

Ripley let out a whoop of support.

Imogen paled. "Fine," she gritted out through clenched teeth.

"Okay, my first question is a clarifying one. You think Damien messed with the light on purpose to frame Winnie for Francine's death and get her fired?" I asked. "Because she was blackmailing Petra?"

Could that be the fight the two of them had last week? It would make sense. Well, I didn't know if I truly believed Winnie was capable of blackmailing someone, but I suppose I was learning that a lot of things weren't quite what they seemed.

Hands flying up in the air—one still clutching the sewing kit while the other held the dress—Imogen said, "I'm just calling what I see. Winnie was afraid of heights, so Damien often did her light checks for her. Damien was the one who sent Francine to clean the sticky mess on the stage left over by that tape. He knew she'd be in one spot for a few minutes, at least."

"The sticky spot on the stage," I said, the words breathy. The spot Carter had stepped on the other day after Don had peeled the tape up that had acted as his anchor during that first rehearsal I'd watched. "But why would Francine clean that up? Wouldn't that be something Damien usually took care of?"

"Exactly." Imogen touched the delicate tip of her nose. "Why *would* Damien send Francine to do that?"

Anger heated in my neck, moving up into my face. He'd lied to me. He'd said he had no idea why Francine had been on the stage yesterday.

"As for the blackmail," Imogen continued, "I honestly don't know what Winnie had on Petra." Her jaw clenched as if it bothered her to admit that she didn't know all the details. "All I know is that Petra and Winnie got into a huge argument, that Winnie said she knew something that could ruin Petra's reputation if she didn't do what she asked."

"Reputation?" The interest building inside me fell flat. That didn't seem like a good enough reason to send someone drugged chocolates.

Imogen lifted her chin. "Oh, don't underestimate what Petra would do to keep her reputation. That woman is all about how others see her, *especially* now that she's in the running for a seat on the board of that arts charity she and her rich friends support." Imogen must've seen that I didn't understand, because she didn't even wait for me to ask a follow-up question before she explained. "Petra's goal for the last, oh, ten years, has been to be the financial chair for an organization that ensures arts programs are available in low-income neighborhoods. It's her *crowning achievement, the biggest feather in her cap she could hope for*. Her words, not mine."

"And whatever blackmail Winnie threatened her with was enough to jeopardize that dream?" I guessed.

"It must've been. That's the only thing I can think that would've gotten Petra's attention, other than if someone threatened Yas or Damien." Imogen picked at a nail as if she might be bored with this conversation. "If her integrity was called into question, the board might vote in someone else's favor, ruining all her hard work."

"This place is terrible." The fury that had been building inside me during the conversation simmered into sadness. I wasn't sure about Penny's suspicion that the place was cursed, but it was definitely a toxic atmosphere. I turned toward the makeshift door.

"Make sure she puts that costume back before you leave, Megs." There was fire in Ripley's eyes as she eyed Imogen.

"Don't think I forgot about that dress either. If I hear anything about Yas not fitting into her costumes, I'll be the first to let her know why that is." The words spilled out of me, making me sick. What right did I have to get mad at them for blackmailing one another when I was willing to do it too? Was I any better than the rest of them?

"Oh, don't give me that." Imogen swatted the air in my direction but ripped the thread she'd been sewing into the dress instead of adding another stitch. She placed the costume back on the rack. "This is just how we are. Last month, Yasmine had Damien saw about an inch off all my heels so I kept tottering over, and then she started a rumor that I was drinking on the job. It's showbiz." Checking her watch, she said, "It's almost my scene. I've got to go." With that, she turned on her heel and left.

"Not the kind of showbiz I want to be involved with," I muttered under my breath, but I left, too, hearing the stomping of feet coming up the staircase signaling that more of the cast would be coming in soon.

When I got back to the prop room, however, it looked like I wasn't going to get to work again just yet. Ripley's face was a mask of frustration.

"What's up?" I asked. Learning that Yasmine and Damien were bigger suspects than we'd first realized was good for our case, not bad. The information didn't warrant the expression she was sporting.

"Get out your phone." Ripley snapped her fingers at me.

The sharp command made me itch to defy her, to push back. Curiosity, however, won out, and I brought the thing out of my purse.

"Look up a nineteen nineties' Seattle theatre accident." Ripley chose each word carefully.

I squinted one eye at her, not sure where she was going with this, but willing to follow where she was leading.

"The wardrobe sabotage, starting rumors about one another, bad lighting, blackmail ... all of this fighting sounds familiar." Ripley waited for me to type the words in the search bar.

The results popped up on my screen, and my lungs jolted with the air I rapidly sucked down in my astonishment. Three faces stared back at me from the article from the *Seattle Times*. Katherine, Janet, and Nathanial.

Ripley ran her tongue over her lips. "I thought the three of them seemed familiar. But hearing Imogen talk about all the infighting between cast members made it all click. This happened a couple of years before I died.

I read the article, relaying key points to Ripley, who confirmed that was what she remembered.

"So, Janet and Katherine hated one another so much that they got in a fight onstage." I summarized the information I'd just read aloud. "And when Nathanial, their director, came to break up the fight, it resulted in an accident that toppled the largest set, killing all three of them."

Ripley nodded seriously. "I'd bet you anything that's why those three ghosts can't be in the same space anymore. They already fought to the death once. Now they're stuck in this theatre together for the rest of their afterlife as punishment."

Sixteen

The momentary excitement surrounding Ripley's discovery wore off. "Knowing the truth about the theatre ghosts doesn't help us much with our Winnie case, though. It just proves that they're a lost cause," she said.

"Tell me about it." I huffed, leaning on a stool as I clutched my phone. "I thought they just hated each other, but to cause one another's deaths? That's brutal. No wonder they're stuck here."

"You know," a smooth voice cut through the quiet of the prop room. "It's not nice to talk about people when they can overhear you."

While I jumped at first, my worry softened as I turned to find Katherine standing behind me, a somewhat transparent hand on her hip.

"Sorry if we don't have a map telling us where each of you is allowed to go," Ripley countered with enough attitude that I was glad I wasn't on the receiving end.

Katherine huffed. "Well, I've been trying to stay away now that you two have been hanging around here more, but I couldn't help but catch my name in your conversation."

"You say *hanging around* like we're just goofing off." I scowled in her direction. "I work here."

"Sure." Katherine's eyes narrowed on me. "That's the *only* reason you're here. There's nothing you're trying to find out by sneaking around in people's dressing rooms."

"I thought you weren't allowed in that area." Ripley mirrored the other ghost, putting her hand on her hip as well.

"I heard you talking about it." Katherine cocked an eyebrow. "You really should be more careful. You never know who's going to walk back here and hear you talking to yourself."

"The cast is all busy. No one's coming back here. And if someone does, I'll just tell them I like to talk to myself while I work." Glancing at Ripley for support, I expected to see her nodding in agreement.

Instead, my best friend's face was tight with fear. But she wasn't looking at me, or at Katherine, for that matter. She was looking behind me. My stomach dropped.

"Meg?"

Hearing Laurie's voice usually made me feel safe, at home. At that moment, it sent a rush of pure dread down the backs of my arms.

I spun around. "Laurie, hey. When did you get here? What are you doing? Are you on a lunch break?"

"What are you trying to do, drown him in questions, Megs?" Ripley cut out.

He held up a to-go bag of food to prove I'd guessed right with my final question. "I thought we could have lunch together."

I stepped toward him. "Sure. I'm starving. Let's do it."

But as I grabbed on to his arm and attempted to walk out of the prop room, Laurie stayed put. Cringing, I fixed my face into a neutral expression before turning around.

"Meg, who were you talking to just now?" Laurie asked.

Heat flushed up my neck and into my cheeks. "Oh, that?" I laughed. "I was just talking to myself. I do that when I paint sometimes."

A muscle in his jaw tightened. "That's what you *said* you'd tell people if they caught you." His voice was level, still Laurie, but I could see something brewing behind his eyes, like a storm on the horizon. "Who'd you say that to?"

I'd spent the entire morning alone in the prop room, but of course, at that moment, Damien chose to walk in from the stage. The large barn-style door had been pushed open a few feet so he could slip through, probably to grab a prop for rehearsal. I marveled at the quietness of the door but figured it would need to be well-oiled in case they needed to retrieve something from this room during a show.

Laurie, less focused on the silent door and more on the gorgeous man standing behind me, cleared his throat. "Him? Were you talking to him? Why would you need to hide that?"

Damien, as he was wont to do, stayed silent. He didn't come to my aid to tell Laurie that he had only just walked into the room.

"Are you seeing him?" Irritation burned in Laurie's question. "Is that why you're trying to hide it? Hide *him*?"

"No." The word was folded up in a desperate plea. "It's not like that. I don't know why he's here."

"What is it like, then, Meg? If it wasn't him, who were you talking to when I walked in?"

A surge of anger rushed into my brain. "You're really going to come in here and accuse me of seeing someone else? I was talking to myself," I insisted.

"Again with that lie." Laurie exhaled a biting laugh. "You really think I'm dense enough not to see when you're lying to me, Meg? It's been happening all week. I thought it was about something smaller, but I guess now I know why you've been secretive when you talk about the theatre. You had to cover up the fact that you're seeing this guy behind my back."

"You really think I'm the cheating type?" I asked, aware that I was sidestepping his accusation about the lies I'd been telling him.

Putting up the hand that wasn't clutching the bag of food, Laurie took a step back. "You know what? This was a bad idea."

"What was a bad idea? Lunch or us?"

Anger simmered in his eyes. "Both. I obviously made a mistake when I said I knew you. I have no idea who you are right now, and I don't care to stick around to find out."

The sharpness to his tone should've cut me to the bone. It should've made tears spring to my eyes. Laurie and I had fought before, sure, but never like this—never like we hated each other. But that's what I felt as Laurie stormed out of the prop room.

When I turned around, Damien was gone as well.

"Jerk," I muttered.

"You referring to Damien, Laurie, or yourself there, Megs?" Ripley's voice cut from the other side of the room, her tone full of malice.

I balked at her question. "Ouch," I said. "You're one to talk. You've been awful to be around all week."

Ripley pulled a hurt face at my words. At first, I thought she might be about to cry, but then she gasped and pointed at Katherine. I didn't notice anything different that might warrant such a response. The ghost looked just like she had minutes before. In fact, she was still even in the same stance, hand on her hip, an air of superiority surrounding her.

"It's *you*." Ripley's eyes were wide.

That made Katherine stagger back half a step. "What's me?" She bit out the question, but her gaze faltered, too, flicking to me and then back to Ripley.

Ripley turned toward me and motioned to the door Laurie had just walked through. "That was *not* the Laurie we know and love. Meg, you've been angry and paranoid, biting people's heads off over the littlest things. I didn't figure it out at first because it's not unusual for the two of us to get at each other's throats. But you and Laurie? You never talk like you just did. And you said yourself that I've been crafty, coming up with plans that have no regard for people's feelings, even yours."

Now that my anger was subsiding, I started to see the fight Laurie and I just had more clearly. It was like I'd been in a fog of rage, and it wasn't the first time I'd felt that this week. Now I could see it for what it was: completely uncharacteristic for both of us. He wasn't jealous, and I wasn't a liar. Well, I might be a *slight* liar—but usually I could explain myself a little better than I just had. Regardless, Laurie getting jealous of Damien for no reason? That wasn't the man I'd fallen for.

"What are you saying, Ripley?" My voice shook as I glanced over at Katherine. "What do you think she's doing?"

But instead of looking smug, like I would expect a spirit to look if they were doing something evil, Katherine looked worried. Scared, even. Catching herself, Katherine covered the fear with that same indifference I'd seen minutes ago.

"Their bad attitudes ... it got them killed, and now it's infecting the whole cast and crew." Ripley paced as she whispered to herself, working it out as she did so. "It's like the river of slime."

"River of slime?" I coughed.

"This is preposterous." Katherine moved like she was going to turn away.

"The river of slime." Ripley opened her hands as if it should make sense. "*Ghostbusters II*."

Katherine and I shared a confused look, and I hated to admit it, but I was kind of on her side with the whole *preposterous* business.

Ripley exhaled loudly as if disappointed that she had to explain. "There's a river of pink slime running through the sewers of New York City, created by the bad vibes in the city, but if anyone comes into contact with it, they become especially terrible." She flapped her hand toward Katherine. "You and I both felt a weird energy here the moment we stepped foot inside the theatre, but the only times we've fought with one another is when one of them is nearby."

The way I'd felt irritated with Ripley. My paranoia

surrounding Francine's death, and how I worried the cast thought it had been my fault. The anger toward Yasmine and Imogen that made me ask blunt questions. The suspicion I'd felt when Laurie had been standing in front of me. It all made sense now.

I was back on Ripley's side. "The curse! It's real." When Ripley wrinkled her forehead in confusion, I added, "Both Winnie and Penny mentioned this theatre being cursed. Penny said it was doing well, and then suddenly, it started to tank. She mentioned that it's been struggling for decades. I'm guessing since 1997. And Laurie…" I covered my mouth with my hand. "Hold on." I pulled out my phone and typed out a quick message.

> I'm so sorry. I promise I can explain.

He wrote back immediately.

> I'm sorry too. I don't know what came over me. I got a call from work right after I left so I can't come back right now, but later?

Breathing a sigh of relief, I responded.

> Later sounds great.

With that taken care of, I turned back to the ghosts.
"Everything okay?" Ripley asked.
I smiled thinly at her. "I think it will be. Okay, so your theory is that the negative energy the three of them are

constantly sending out is rubbing off on us?" I asked, making sure I was understanding correctly.

Katherine huffed. "Insulting."

But Ripley didn't pay any attention to her. She said, "It's even more than that, and it's not just us. Remember that story about how they died? Their jealousy, paranoia, and general bad attitudes got all three of them killed. The article mentioned that there had been bad history between Janet and Katherine." She turned to the ghost. "Katherine, that wouldn't have included things like altering one another's costumes to make the other think she's put on weight or arranging for the lighting to be unflattering during a showing where you know a critic is going to be in attendance?"

Katherine drove out a harsh breath, but she didn't deny any of it.

Ripley laughed triumphantly. "I knew it. The bad vibes from these three are rubbing off on the current cast and crew."

My lungs jerked back into action after a beat. "And I'd bet anything Nathanial was the kind of director who yelled all the time and scared people into doing what he wanted. I'd bet that even though he ran up there to break up that fight between you two, he'd actually encouraged the competition, just like Carter does."

"Oh, good point." Ripley nodded. "I'd been wondering why Nathanial was here too, if it was mostly about Katherine and Janet, but I'd bet he fed their rivalry and added to the negative atmosphere. He had to have been an equal participant if he's stuck here too."

"Had to," I agreed. "And now he's turning Carter into the same kind of director."

Katherine muttered something unintelligible and turned away.

Ripley smiled at me. "This place isn't cursed. It's just got a river of slime running through it in the form of three ghosts who died because of their jealousy and pettiness."

That comment acted as some sort of breaking point for Katherine. She stalked over to Ripley. "I will have you know that…" But she didn't finish that statement.

It was as if her anger became so intense, so overwhelming, that she couldn't speak. If she could've, I think she would've turned red. The ghost clenched her teeth and then, just when I thought she might take a swing at Ripley, the ghost disappeared instead.

"So much for taking responsibility for your actions," Ripley muttered.

But before I could add anything, Katherine reappeared. A confused Janet and Nathanial stood next to her.

Seventeen

"Go ahead." Katherine flapped a hand toward Ripley. "Tell them what you said to me, about the slime." The disgust still laced her tone, but there was an air of ... regret hanging around her spirit that I hadn't seen before.

I think I only noticed it in contrast to Janet and Nathanial. They wore indifferent expressions to match Katherine's previous attitude. But now, Katherine's eyes tightened ever so slightly, as if she might be experiencing grief.

"You're all toxic," Ripley said, pulling zero punches.

I winced. "Okay, well, that might not be the best way to start." Stepping forward, I patted the air with my hands. "Janet, Nathanial, we know how the three of you died."

The ghosts shared a worried glance before turning back to me. Nathanial, at least, had the decency to look embarrassed. Janet simply folded her arms and tilted her head.

"Correct me if I'm wrong," I prefaced, because maybe the journalist who wrote the news article hadn't been privy to all the details. "But Katherine and Janet, the two of you were in a production of *The Music Man* in 1997. Nathanial was the director, of course."

"Of course," he scoffed. "And we died. End of story."

Ripley shot him a glower and took over. "*Not* the end of the story. After months of Janet and Katherine sabotaging one another in smaller, less-destructive ways—encouraged by their director—their rivalry reached a critical moment on closing night. Janet shoved Katherine during one of the big dance numbers near the end of the show."

"She shoved me first!" Janet stepped forward.

Katherine rolled her eyes. "I did not, you psychopath."

"Hey!" Ripley's voice cut through the fighting. "It doesn't matter who started it. The two of you got in a literal fistfight on stage, in front of an audience. Katherine, you saw the trapdoor opening for the next scene and tried to push Janet down it. Nathanial, you jumped up there to try to stop it all, but not only did you *not* grab Janet in time, but you fell back into one of the largest props, causing it to fall on you and Katherine, crushing you both instantly. Janet, you died landing wrong at the bottom of the trapdoor."

"Yes." Janet looked down.

Her attitude wasn't the only one that was tempered in the face of those details.

"That was all ... accurate," Katherine whispered.

"Well, you know what else is accurate?" Ripley's attitude ramped up as she grew tired of the three ghosts. "You didn't leave that toxicity behind. Your bad vibes are affecting every person in this building."

"You're why Imogen and Yasmine are at each other's

throats constantly," I said. "Why Francine and Winnie were constantly fighting over the light-booth job. Why Carter's only form of communication is yelling."

"And you're likely responsible for a ton of smaller squabbles over the years." Ripley wagged her head like a disappointed mother even though she appeared years, if not decades, younger than the other spirits. "You're why I've had no regard for anyone else's feelings or safety all week, why Meg's only emotions have been anger and paranoia, and why her sweet boyfriend just came in here acting like a jealous jerk." She set a fist on her hip to punctuate the end of her point.

For a tense moment, I thought the ghosts wouldn't own up to any of it, that we'd be stuck with this toxic environment forever, and it really would take the theatre down with it.

Nathanial's eyes narrowed. "Come to think of it, that makes sense. Yasmine and Imogen definitely remind me of these two." He motioned to Katherine and Janet. "And I thought history was going to repeat itself during the show they just finished."

"How so?" I asked.

"Before *Singing in the Rain* the Third Avenue did a production of *Newsies*."

"It was actually an all-female production, so Yasmine and Imogen were the two leads," Katherine corrected.

"*Jaclyn* Kelly and *Daveny* Jacobs." Imogen smiled at the female versions of the main characters' names.

"That's pretty awesome," Ripley conceded. "I love that movie."

I agreed, but turned my attention back to Nathanial to hear the end of his story.

"Yasmine and Imogen almost looked like they were going to get in a fight on stage," he explained. "It happened during 'Seize the Day.' It's supposed to be this uplifting number, and it was a disaster. Luckily, Carter was able to separate them before anyone was hurt, but it felt eerily similar to how it happened with all of us." He looked to his fellow theatre ghosts.

Janet's chest expanded as it would've if she'd actually had lungs to take in a full inhale. "Fine. Maybe you're right. What are we supposed to do about it?"

Ripley looked to me for the answer. I expected the same surge of irritation to overcome me as it had yesterday when Ripley tried to pass the conversation to me. But it didn't come. It seemed as though even the small change these ghosts had made in just admitting that they were the problem was already having an effect.

"I think this is your unfinished business," I said. "It's why the three of you are stuck here in this theatre. It's not normal for spirits to be contained inside one building. You should be able to wander anywhere you set foot while you were alive. The universe is trying to tell you to fix your relationship with one another and fix the damage you've done here in the Third Avenue."

I couldn't help but notice the way Ripley's shoulders hunched in discomfort. Right. Unfinished business wasn't a comfortable topic for her at the moment.

"What do you want us to do?" Katherine's words were sharp with annoyance.

"Help me figure out who's trying to kill Winnie," I said, unsure if the pleading tone in my voice would help or hurt my case with the ghosts. "Help us figure out, for sure, what really happened to Francine, if that light really did just fall on her by accident or if someone dropped it on her."

Suddenly, over the intercom, I heard, "Second call for Miss Meg, the artist. Carter would like to see you on the stage."

Second call? I must've missed the first while arguing with the ghosts.

"You go," Ripley said, waving me off. "We'll work this out."

I fixed my best friend with a grateful look before leaving for the stage. At first when Carter patted the seat beside him where he sat in the audience, watching the rehearsal, I thought he was going to make me sit through the rest of the play like he had my first day, talking about props. Luckily, he just wanted an update about my progress with the sets. Once he was satisfied that everything was on its way, he let me go.

I pushed my way through the prop room door and found the four ghosts just where I'd left them. The three theatre ghosts were talking over one another, but nowhere near to the extent, or with the venom, that I'd experienced last time we'd tried to force them to have a conversation.

It seemed that Ripley had them going through all the cast and crew, looking for common threads that might lead us to information about who wanted Winnie dead. I got to work painting the second flat, listening to the ghosts as they talked about everyone. They also knew Damien was in love with Yasmine, as well as Yasmine being Petra's daughter. Janet hadn't heard the end of Carter's phone conversation with Petra, and none of them had any idea what blackmail Winnie might have on her.

"Yasmine and Imogen got into it over Petra all the time. I swear Yasmine spends half her time defending Petra from different allegations," Janet said, letting her head loll back as if it were the most tedious thing.

"Like what?" Ripley asked.

Katherine held up ghostly fingers as she gave an answer in the form of a list. "They don't think she's invested in this theatre anymore. She spends less and less time here each production. They want her to sell it. Some are mad that she keeps letting Carter direct, and others feel like she doesn't do enough to keep him happy. They're mad that all she seems to care about is how her rich friends see her. Even Francine, who used to be solidly on Petra's side, had started to turn against her."

"Especially after Petra gave Winnie the lighting-booth job and moved Francine to concessions," Janet added.

Katherine agreed. "Before that, Petra was one of the only people Francine seemed to like. Francine butted heads with everyone. She and Winnie fought all the time. She and Carter couldn't stand one another."

"She reamed out Carter the other day because he signed for a shipment of candy, and she said the inventory was off by one box of chocolates." Nathanial snorted. "Can you imagine? Getting so upset about one box?"

Perking up, I was about to ask if maybe the missing box was the fancy donor chocolates, but the barn-style door leading to the stage slid open again. It seemed Damien was back to collect whatever props he'd come to get earlier when Laurie was here, and I had to keep my mouth shut.

Little did Francine know that Carter didn't mess up the inventory; someone stole that box of chocolates with the intention of killing Winnie, I thought to myself as the ghosts moved on to talking about a fight Francine got in with Don about holding tickets for his family at the door.

With the sporadic interruptions, I focused on listening and working. And I must've lost myself in the painting because hours had passed the next time I checked the time.

In my brain, I held a whole catalog of everything the ghosts had said about the theatre and the people who worked here. Yasmine left early on Tuesdays for voice lessons. Damien had a criminal record but it was from when he was a minor, before Petra took him in, and as far as they knew he hadn't had any run-ins with the law since. Carter must be worried about this production because any moment they weren't rehearsing he had earbuds in his ears. When people asked what he was listening to, he said it was the musical soundtrack on repeat. Imogen was a twin, and her sister was the lead at the Fifth Avenue's recent run of *Into the Woods*, which was probably part of why she put so much pressure on herself.

The biggest revelation was that the ghosts had noticed Damien and Yasmine sneaking around, whispering, and looking generally worried as of late. None of them knew the reasoning behind the change in behavior, but they made it their mission to find out.

My phone beeped with a text as I wiped my hands on my overalls. It was from Laurie.

Dinner?

Ripley, having seen the text, met my gaze.

"I need to go. I have to talk to him."

"Of course you do," she assured me. "I think we should all take a break anyway." She glanced over at the other ghosts, noticing that they were trying not to fight, but patience was wearing thin. "I have some stuff to take care of."

"Do we go back to our sections?" Janet asked, glancing at the other two spirits.

Trying not to get caught up in the questions running through my mind about what Ripley's *stuff* was, I said, "That's up to you three. If you need your space, you could, but I think in order to figure out this unfinished business, you need to be able to be in the same areas without being at each other's throats."

Grabbing my jacket and purse, I wandered out into the cool evening air. After texting Laurie back that I was changing and would be ready soon, he sent me an address for a restaurant, telling me he'd be there in half an hour. It all felt a little odd, especially since we lived in the same building and could very well have just walked there together. But after our fight today, I didn't question it. Maybe he needed space.

Back at the Morrisey, the Conversationalists smiled broadly, calling out greetings as I passed by their seating area. Art and Darius were having quite the discussion about the show *M*A*S*H*. Actually, it sounded more like they were just reciting their favorite lines and describing key scenes from the show, but it put a smile on my face, nonetheless. Opal, mostly focused on her book of puzzles, interjected every few seconds with the name of an actor or the title of a movie the other two couldn't seem to remember. George was gone, but that wasn't a surprise this close to the holiday. His family lived in the city still, and I knew he liked to go watch them, especially when he knew they would be gathered together.

As I rushed up the stairs to my apartment, the events of the day were spinning in my head. The gossip we'd learned from the ghosts, now that they were actually talking and we had the benefit of all three of their points of view, became a looming pile in my mind. It felt like I'd put off doing laundry for far too long and the result was daunting, leaving me unsure of where to begin.

Still, I was sure the piece of information we needed was in there somewhere; I just had to figure out what it was.

Eighteen

Changing out of my paint-spattered overalls, I brushed my hair and typed the address Laurie had sent me into my phone. It would only take me ten minutes to walk there, so I took a moment to put a little blush on my cheeks and swipe some mascara over my lashes.

Then I spent my remaining five minutes snuggling Anise on the couch before giving her some fresh food and water.

As I walked, my mind wandered to Ripley, and I wondered about the "stuff" she'd had to do tonight. The fact that she hadn't offered up the information made me jump to the conclusion that it was about her own unfinished business. Maybe she'd already had something planned, but it was possible talking to the Third Avenue Theatre ghosts about the reason they hadn't moved on had sparked some urgency in her.

A deep breath cleared the worst of the worry from my mind. She'd open up to me about it all at some point. I was sure of it. The city sparkled in the frosty November evening.

Laughter and music spilled out of cozy restaurants each time a door opened as I passed by. Condensation plumed in front of me after each exhale, convincing me to pick up the pace so I would arrive at my own destination faster.

A few minutes later, I stopped in front of a taqueria near the waterfront. I'd never even seen the place before. Leave it to Laurie to know the city better than me, though. While I'd been away for years, he'd been here. Granted, the University of Washington was up north, across Lake Union and the bridge from downtown, but I could just see college-aged Laurie driving around the city with his friends on weekends, finding gems like this down side streets and alleys.

Laurie sat at one of the tables near the front of the restaurant. He stood as I entered. Relief flooded through me as I recognized none of the malice from our earlier conversation at the theatre in his expression or body language.

"Hey," he said, pulling me into a tight hug.

I let myself sink into him, the scent of his cologne filling my nose as I pressed my face into his shoulder.

"I'm so sorry," he said as I finally stepped back.

I peeled out of my jacket. "No, I am." Setting it on the back of the chair across from him, I gestured for him to sit. "It was—" I started to say, but then realized that I couldn't tell him what had actually happened today at the theatre, what had been happening to anyone who spent any length of time in the Third Avenue over the past two and a half decades, ever since the toxic trio died on stage in the middle of a performance.

A terrible realization washed over me in that moment. Laurie's jealousy was because of the theatre ghosts and the river of slime they'd created. But he'd been right when he'd said I'd been lying to him all week. That didn't have anything to do with the Third Avenue Theatre or the ghosts who haunted the place. Which meant, that while Laurie's reaction could be explained away as out of character, mine couldn't.

Checking around, I wished for our overeager server from the other night. I needed an interruption, something to take our minds off the current conversation. But there wasn't anyone coming by just yet, and Laurie was waiting for me to finish my sentence about our earlier fight.

"Everyone tells me that place is cursed. I didn't believe them at first, but just being there seems to put people on edge." Puffing out my cheeks, I added, "What's good here?"

Laurie swallowed but followed my lead and looked at the menu. The excitement that had been so palpable, so contagious, moments before, dimmed as he realized everything still wasn't okay. He might not feel the jealousy and paranoia he'd experienced back at the theatre, but he didn't need bad ghostly vibes to tell I was keeping something from him.

After taking a beat to recover, he pointed out a few items he'd tried on the menu and our server came to take our orders. I tried to keep the server there longer, asking questions about different sides I didn't want, to prolong the ordering experience. But eventually, he glanced around, noting another table he needed to visit, and I got the hint that I was taking too long.

I ordered and sat back, blowing out an exhale in the silence that followed. Laurie drew back as he took in my posture.

"Is everything okay?" he asked. "Are you sure you forgive me for how I acted earlier?"

My heart ached as it recognized the confusion so clearly written in Laurie's expression. This was the worst.

"Of course I do," I told him, leaning forward and taking his hand. "I'm sorry, I just had a weird day."

"Want to tell me about it?" The eagerness in his posture felt like a knife to the gut.

I let out a strangled laugh. "Not really. I'd kind of just like to forget about it," I admitted. At least that wasn't a lie.

But the crestfallen look Laurie adopted as he sat back didn't feel like I'd offered him the truth. I couldn't blame him for his frustration. A mounting sense of dread built inside my mind. I'd basically waited my entire life to be in a relationship with this man, and now that I had him, I couldn't ruin it with poor communication.

At that moment, two things happened simultaneously.

Ripley appeared next to our table, wobbling as if she'd been caught off-balance. Her wide eyes took in the restaurant, contracting slightly in recognition as her gaze settled on me.

I'd seen that look before—this whole scene, actually. Ripley must've gone too far. She'd ventured too close to the edge of the tether that kept us together, and it had brought her right back to me. Questions about where she'd been and what she'd been doing so far away should've been rushing through my mind at that moment. They would've been, if not for the second thing that happened.

Laurie, being the observant man that he was, caught my look of surprise. His gaze moved to the space Ripley occupied, to what would seem like emptiness to him, but that I looked quite surprised by.

And I realized that I could either lie to him, yet again, or come clean.

"Laurie, I have something I need to tell you," I blurted out before I could stop myself.

"You do?" Ripley moved closer with interest.

There was a hint of fear hiding in the tightness present in Ripley's question. Even though she'd encouraged me to tell Laurie, I knew she was worried for me, worried about how he would take the news. I shared her fear, but I had to do this.

"Okay," Laurie said, flinching as if he expected me to either slap him across the face or break up with him.

Swallowing any remaining reservations, I leaned close, checked over my shoulders to make sure no one else was within earshot, and said, "There's something about me that you don't know."

He nodded in encouragement, some of the concern in his body language replaced by intrigue.

"I can ... see and converse with ... spirits." I gulped down the rest of the explanation that wanted to come spilling out after those words. I needed to give him a second with that statement first, before I jumped into anything else.

"Converse with? Suddenly, you're formal now?" Ripley joked, and I knew she was trying to get me to lighten up, to take my mind off what Laurie would think of such a declaration.

Laurie's pupils flared, his throat bobbed in a thick swallow, and he scratched at the back of his neck. "Like, ghosts?" he asked in a rough voice.

I croaked out a quiet, "Yep."

He blinked for a few moments, then puffed out his cheeks in a contained exhale. His reaction left me with the itching need to fill the silence.

"It's because of my mom," I said, the words tumbling out of me so fast I couldn't seem to stop them. "Well, because of the accident she was in while she was still pregnant with me. I was around so much death that I guess the ability came to me then because I've always had it. And, Ripley, she was one of the people in the other car who died that day. She's my best friend."

Ripley, who I knew felt as honored to be my friend as I felt being hers, still grimaced at that statement. Telling Laurie my best friend was a ghost would've probably been something best kept until later.

"That's who I was talking to earlier when you came to the theatre," I added.

His eyebrows ticked up at that comment.

I continued, seeing I'd caught his interest. "Well, her, and there are three ghosts who haunt the theatre. They died because they had some inane rivalry, and now they're creating an environment where everyone who spends any length of time in the building is snappy, bitter, and paranoid."

"Like the river of slime," Laurie whispered in awe.

"*Thank* you," Ripley said, beaming at Laurie. "At least someone here has good taste in movies."

"Hey, I have great taste in movies," I retorted before catching myself.

Ripley's eyes widened, and she met my terrified gaze. I'd just spoken to her in front of Laurie. My attention flashed to him, noticing the furrows already present in his brow deepen.

"What was that?" he asked warily. "And what happened right before you told me? Is there a ghost standing here?" He lowered his voice for the final question.

Pressing my lips together, not trusting myself to speak, I simply nodded.

Laurie's forehead relaxed, and his lips pulled into a smile. "This is so cool."

"What?" I asked, coughing in surprise.

Laurie's eyes practically danced with excitement. "You can communicate with the dead. Meg, this is amazing." The earnestness in his tone made it sound like he didn't think I realized any of this.

My lips twitched to the side, wanting to pull into a smile but still wary if they should. "You're not freaked out?"

"Surprised. But not freaked out." Squinting one eye, Laurie said, "Actually, I'm not even all that surprised. I always knew there was something different about you." Clearing his throat, he said, "Not different. Special. You were always so much better at sitting back and observing when we were kids. I admired your ability to stay quiet and listen."

Laurie and his parents hadn't moved into the building until I was five. By that point, I'd learned my lesson about assuming everyone could see the ghosts I was seeing.

Laughing, I told him, "That's not because I'm particularly good at being quiet, it's because I wasn't ever sure which people in a room were alive or not. I got caught out too many times talking to a person no one else could see, so I got used to waiting until I knew for sure if people were still alive."

Sadness pinched at the corners of Laurie's eyes for a brief moment before he whispered, "The nickname that kids at school gave you: NutMeg. That was because they caught you talking to yourself too." It wasn't a question.

By the time Laurie and his parents moved to the building, my beloved Morrisey family had already coined their version of the nickname to help me see it as a good thing instead of something to be teased about. But Laurie went to the same school as I did. He heard the very different version of the nickname the kids called me.

"Yeah. You know how we used to joke that the teachers at school never left the building? Well, it's partly true. That place was filled with the ghosts of past teachers, for one reason or another. My Kindergarten year was filled with me talking to them around my classmates before I wised up."

His mouth quirked up at the corner. "Sorry." He tried, and failed, to wipe the smile from his face. "I'm sad that the other kids were mean to you, but this just explains so much I could never figure out about you, Meg."

"How so?" His smile was contagious, and I found myself fighting a curious grin of my own.

Laurie shrugged. "It's why you're so compassionate. You're constantly talking to people who have sad stories about how they died or why they're still here. It's also why you're so unfailingly brave." He shook his head. "The way you dealt with everything this summer? I was in awe. But, of course you're this fearless when you look death in the face every day." He finally lost the battle with the smile and it grew into a full grin. "You've always seemed so much deeper than anyone else I'd ever met. I knew there was something amazing about you, something that set you apart."

Ripley sighed happily as she glanced from Laurie to me. "I knew he appreciated the real you. I knew he'd be the right one to tell."

I couldn't help but agree with her wholeheartedly.

Our conversation halted as the server came over with our meals, and we focused on eating for a few minutes. I hadn't realized how ravenous I was, but I suppose I'd missed out on lunch because of my fight with Laurie.

He must've caught my earlier glance at Ripley, because he asked, "So, which ghost is here with us now?" Laurie leaned closer, waiting for my answer.

"That would be Ripley." I beamed. "She's the best friend I was telling you about. She's kind of always with me."

He nodded but didn't look like he understood at all.

"We think it's because she died in the accident that took my mom, but her spirit is tied to me. She goes anywhere I go, though she can go a lot farther from me now that I'm older."

"Like a guardian angel." Laurie's mouth tipped upward.

"Exactly."

Ripley might've blushed if she could've. "Tell him I've always appreciated how he saw the real you, Megs. And tell him that I'm so glad you two finally figured things out and kissed."

With more than a modicum of discomfort, I relayed her message to him. Laurie's eyes lit up as he mirrored my reaction. "I think I already like her."

"Well, she's a big fan of you," I said. "So that would make sense."

Taking a bite, Laurie swallowed before saying, "Wait. The cases this summer. Were you able to talk to those ghosts?"

"Not Mr. Miller or Paris Elliott. That's one of the more … inconvenient things about spirits. They don't settle right away, especially if they died in a traumatic way. So, they're not around to answer questions about who killed them. Not that many of them remember exactly how they died anyway." My gaze shifted to Ripley. "It's a defense mechanism, I think. To shield them from going over and over their deaths."

Ripley's mouth jolted into a sad smile. "I think you've got this, Megs." She gave me a quick salute and disappeared.

"Ripley's giving us some privacy now," I told Laurie, who waved adorably at the air next to our table.

As we ate, I explained everything about Addy, the flapper ghost who'd helped me solve Paris Elliott's murder, and how Ripley and George had helped me with Mr. Miller's case.

"Are there just ghosts everywhere?" he asked.

A smile spread across my face as we finished our meals. "Pretty much. Wanna meet some of them?"

Nineteen

Telling Laurie about ghosts was exhilarating. Excitement buzzed through my body as we walked through the city, back toward the Morrisey, leaving me feeling warm despite the frosty temperatures. Or, maybe, that could've been the fact that Laurie had his arm wrapped around my shoulders as we walked, nestling me into his side while he listened to me explain everything I'd learned in my twenty-four years around ghosts.

"Oh, there's one across the street right now," I whispered to Laurie, glancing over at a spirit hanging out in one of the street-side stairwells that would lead into the Underground section of the city. "I can tell because it's kinda sparkly. Ghosts are so much easier to spot in the dark because any light gets caught up in their spirit, making them look like they're glowing. The effect is especially pretty when it comes to moonlight."

"So, the movies got that part right," Laurie said. "How about their voices? Are they all slow and faraway sounding?"

Laughing at the silliness of that myth, I told him, "Only when they use too much of their energy at once and they go *sketchy*, as Ripley likes to call it."

"But they have energy? They can make things move in our world?"

"To a certain extent. It's wildly inconsistent and mostly tied to their emotions, but yes, they can make doors slam shut, stuff like that, no problem."

Having arrived in the small, triangular park in front of our building, I spotted the Squares hanging out by the pergola and called them over. They balked at first, seeing Laurie by my side, but I gave them an extra beckoning gesture to show them it was okay.

At any given moment, the group of Squares might range from three to twelve ghosts. That night, it was on the larger end with ten. Because of the size, I did a quick round of introductions, trying to give Laurie a little background about each ghost, along with their name.

"There are a lot of you from the early nineteen hundreds," Laurie observed with an eyebrow raise.

The ghosts laughed and Victor said, "It was a dangerous time. Fun, but dangerous."

I relayed his message to Laurie, who joined in on their laughter. Then we said our goodbyes as we sauntered toward the Morrisey.

Stopping me before we went inside, Laurie said, "They all seem so nice. Have you ever met any scary ghosts?"

"A few." Cold pricked at my skin despite my closeness to Laurie as I thought about those individuals. "In fact, some of them are in our building."

I explained about the basement ghosts, how they ran an old prohibition era gambling hall that used to be under the Morrisey, how they'd scared me and Penny when I was younger. But I also explained how they'd helped me with Addy's and Paris's cases this past summer.

"No wonder I could never get you to go into the basement." He chuckled, but then stopped. "Wait. The ghosts scared you and Penny in the basement. Does she know? Who else? Zoe?"

Swallowing, I explained. "Penny just thought the basement was creepy and that one of the boxes had been stacked wrong so that's why it fell. Actually, no one else knows. You're the first."

Laurie blinked, staying silent for a moment.

"I was always worried that people would think I was losing my mind, that they wouldn't believe me, or they would see me differently after I told them," I admitted.

His brown eyes softened, and his hand came up to cup my face. "I'm glad you trusted me. Thank you." He leaned down and kissed me.

I didn't want that to stop, but a round of whistles rang out. At first, I wondered if it might be the Squares, who we'd just left behind, but it was coming from inside the Morrisey. Laurie heard it, too, because he craned his neck to see what the commotion was.

And that's when we realized our mistake.

The Conversationalists, including Opal, Nancy, and even George, were standing in the lobby of the Morrisey, waving and cheering. They wore huge smiles and were beckoning us to come inside.

Cheeks heating, I glanced over at Laurie. His mouth pulled into an awkward smile and he tugged me closer.

"Well, I guess that's what I get for giving in to the urge to kiss you without thinking about where we are," he said into my hair. "Should we go inside?"

Laughing, I said, "Sure. They'll be worse if we don't."

Another round of cheers erupted from the small group as we entered the building. Nancy rushed forth, taking us each by the hand and pulling us forward as if she were about to marry us. Instead, she pushed us onto one of the couches.

"When did this happen?" she asked, punctuating each word with a clap of her hands.

Laurie rubbed the back of his neck. "Pretty recently, actually."

Opal took a crisply indrawn breath. "Don't tell me that was your first kiss that we just interrupted?"

I coughed. "Nope. Not our first."

"Did everyone else know Laurence was back from Japan?" Art asked, scratching his head.

"You saw him the other day," Opal said, punctuating the statement with an eye roll.

Art squinted one eye. "Are you sure that wasn't a couple of months ago?"

"Obviously." Nancy gestured to Laurie, sitting right in front of them. "Now, let's get back to the two of you being an item." She shimmied her shoulders.

"Not much to tell," Laurie said. "You all know I've been crazy about Meg forever. I finally worked up the courage to ask her out." He shrugged, like he hadn't just said something that made my heart melt.

"Oh, we knew *both* of you were crazy about one another," Nancy told us. "We actually had a pool going of who was going to ask who out first, but we stopped once you left for the East Coast, Nutmeg."

Snapping his fingers, Darius said, "Wait, Meg, you weren't the first one to make a move, were you? Because, if so, I think I might be a very rich man." His eyes shone with the possibility.

I laughed, loving Darius for believing I might have the courage to ask Laurie out first. "Nope. Sorry. It was all Laurie."

Laurie's lips pulled into a side smile. "Well, not *all* me. We can say fifty-fifty."

Darius lit up. "Does that mean I get half the money since I'm the only one who voted for Nutmeg?"

"No, Darius," Nancy retorted. "We threw out the pool, remember?"

"I wasn't around when you two were younger *nor* was I part of any pool," Opal said, lifting her chin as if she was above any of the pettiness. "But you're just adorable together, and I'm glad you're so happy."

Laurie inclined his head. "Thank you."

"Yes, thanks, Opal," I said, standing. I grabbed Laurie's hand, tugging him off the couch and toward the staircase. It seemed like a good time to make a break for it, or we were going to be here for hours.

As we bid the group goodbye, I caught George's eye and jerked my head toward the elevator, hoping he'd follow. He did, though his movements were cautious at first, seeing I was still with Laurie. The ghost entered the elevator with us, narrowing his eyes at me as he waited.

"George," I said once the elevator doors closed.

His eyes flew open, and he glanced at Laurie, who wasn't quite sure where to look but was trying to keep his expression open.

Quickly moving to an explanation, I added, "I told Laurie about my ability to talk to all of you, and I wanted to formally introduce you."

Blinking, George said, "But, Nutmeg, you haven't told anyone ... ever."

"I know. It was time that I let someone in, and I couldn't lie to Laurie any longer." I didn't bother repeating what George had said to Laurie, figuring he could guess based on my answer.

George's surprise morphed into happiness. "I'm glad. I think it'll be good for you to have someone else to talk to. Tell him he's a lucky man."

I begrudgingly repeated the compliment for Laurie.

His eyes flashed with a smile. "Oh, don't worry, George. I'm well-aware."

The elevator dinged open on the fifth floor, and we told George we'd see him around, though technically only I would. Then we stopped by my place to grab blankets before wandering up onto the roof to talk more.

"Are there any ghosts up here?" Laurie whispered as we stepped into the frosty November air.

Nodding gravely, my attention went to the left where the figure of Rooftop Rachel floated, just as she always had.

"Ripley and I call her Rooftop Rachel, but we have no idea what her name is or where she came from. She never talks. Never moves. Just floats right over there in the corner, gazing out toward Elliott Bay and the Puget Sound beyond that.

"Creepy." Laurie ran a hand over his arm as if to get rid of goosebumps.

I tipped up one shoulder. "A little bit. Mostly I feel bad for her. She just always seems so sad."

There were lights we could've plugged in, but given that we were one of the shorter buildings, the tall skyscrapers around us emitted enough ambient light that we could see the outline of the furniture and planters. We opted to leave the lights off as we moved over toward the firepit we'd purchased as a building a few months ago.

Laurie turned it on while I grabbed the cushions for the love seat out of the storage shed where they lived during the rainy months of the year. Once both tasks were done, we plopped onto the love seat together, snuggling in close. Laurie's arm and blanket wrapped around me, and I leaned my head on his chest as I watched the flames.

"What do they look like?" he whispered, probably worried Rooftop Rachel might overhear. "Like, are they bloody?"

"Based on everything I've seen, spirits manifest as their truest self. They might not even look exactly how they did when they died if they felt more at home during another part of their life."

I explained to him a time I'd met a ghost who appeared to be a teenager. I'd been sad, thinking she'd died so young, but she told me that she'd actually lived a long life, but it was very hard and she'd dealt with addiction—the thing that eventually killed her—so the last time she'd felt truly herself was when she was younger.

"That's kind of beautiful," he said, then shuddered. "But I cannot imagine going back to being an awkward teenager."

"Oh, gosh, no. Most people are comfortable with who they are at any given time, so that's why they appear closest to the age they were when they died. They also don't have to wear the clothes they died in." I told him all about Ripley, how she'd died in a terribly short and tight black dress, and yet her ghost clothing was her usual grunge band T-shirt, cutoff shorts, black tights, boots, and flannel.

That sparked so many questions about Ripley, specifically. Laurie wanted to know how she died, what she was like, and what her unfinished business was. I told him everything, my smile growing as I described my tough, grunge-loving, stubborn best friend. I also explained our theories surrounding why Ripley was still here and how she'd been looking into it recently, hence her secrecy about where she'd been when she was pulled back to my side this evening during dinner.

We talked for an hour, maybe more. After a while, we turned off the fire, not wanting to use up all the propane. I met Laurie's gaze in the light of the city.

"Thank you," I whispered.

He tucked a piece of my hair behind my ear. "For what?"

"I don't know why I expected anything different, but you've made me feel so comfortable telling you all of this. And I can't even tell you how good it is to have someone else who knows." I leaned forward and kissed him.

And kissed him.

I stopped before I climbed into his lap.

He let out a hoarse chuckle. "Any other secrets you want to tell me? I'll hear them all if it means you kiss me like that."

I swatted him on the arm. "Seriously, Laurie. It's not every day someone tells you that they can commune with the dead. You're not giving yourself credit for how great you're taking all of this."

Swallowing, Laurie turned serious. "I think it's because it's you. If anyone else had told me the same thing, I might've reacted a lot different. But ... it's you. I trust you, Meg." He kissed my forehead, then my nose, then my mouth.

Self-control was overrated. I was getting in his lap.

I was about to make my move when Ripley appeared in front of us. "Meg? Are you up here?" She held her hand in front of her eyes.

"Oh, yeah. I'm here," I said, turning to Laurie, and whispering, "Ripley."

He nodded.

"Why are you covering your eyes, Rip?" I asked with a giggle.

"Because I wasn't sure what I'd be interrupting." She slowly lowered her hand, peering out at us. Seeing that everything was safe, she relaxed.

"Who do you think we are, Ripley? Exhibitionists?" Laurie asked with a chuckle, motioning to the dozens of buildings surrounding us, many of which were taller than ours and therefore looked out over the rooftop.

Love for him swelled inside me. He'd spoken directly to Ripley instead of asking me to relay the message to her. For some reason, that made his acceptance feel even more genuine.

She laughed. "Touché."

I relayed her answer to him, smiling at the fact that my two best friends were finally getting to talk to one another.

"So?" I asked. "What's up?"

It wasn't as if I wasn't happy to see her, but there were *other* things on my mind at that moment.

Ripley's eyes went wide and she stepped forward. "Oh, right. Um, I have some big news from the theatre ghosts."

"The theatre ghosts?" I asked. "You went back?"

"I did. They took a break from each other, but when I returned, they were kind of stuck on the relationship between Winnie, and Francine, and ... well, it's not good."

I gulped, repeating what Ripley said for Laurie. After I was done, I said, "Hit us with it." I preemptively cringed.

"'K. Here it goes. When I brought up the chocolates Winnie had received in the mail, they remembered chocolates being used as a weapon, of sorts, before."

"Really? That's amazing." I looked at Laurie, filling him in on what she'd said.

But when I turned my attention back to Ripley, she was shaking her head. "It's not good news. The only other person they can remember sending tampered chocolates to another person is Winnie."

Twenty

"Winnie?" I asked, my throat feeling suddenly dry. "Winnie sent someone poisoned chocolates before?" I repeated, filling in the information in case Laurie was lost.

He let out a weighty exhale.

"Well, she didn't *poison* the ones she sent." Ripley held up her index finger. "She added some kind of laxative to hers, so it was more an inconvenience than an attempt on someone's life, but ... yeah." Ripley bared her teeth.

"Who'd she send them to?" Laurie asked. "The person could've sent these in retribution."

"That's kind of like running someone over with your car in response to them stepping on your toe, but I guess," I said, shaking my head.

Ripley ignored my comment, siding with Laurie. "The ghosts think it could be exactly what Laurie said: retribution. Obviously more than just the chocolate incident in the past went into this decision, but the fact is, the person she sent the chocolates to was Yasmine."

"Yasmine?" I asked, quickly changing my vote to the retribution side.

"Who's she?" Laurie asked.

"Yasmine is not only one of the leads in the current musical," I explained, "but she's also the daughter of the woman who owns the theatre, who we believe Winnie could've been blackmailing, and who Winnie got in a big fight with last week. We're not sure what kind of blackmail Winnie has on Petra, but Yasmine and Damien seemed to know about it."

"Tell him about Damien." Ripley fluttered her hands in front of herself.

"Oh, right. That guy, Damien, who you 'met' today." I used finger quotes around the word since meeting Damien was about as formal as saying you'd been introduced to a wolf who watched you from the woods as you walked through a forest at night. "Well, Petra's like a foster mom to him, and he's also been in love with Yasmine for ages. He had access to the lights because Winnie made him go up on the catwalk since she was scared of heights."

"And you think he could've sent the chocolates to Winnie to keep Petra safe and to get revenge for the chocolates Winnie sent to Yasmine years ago?" Laurie guessed.

"I think the chocolates might've been Yasmine. Remember that frog sticker on the card? I found one of the same ones on multiple items in Yasmine's dressing room. Maybe she and Damien are working together." I let my head fall back in fatigue. "But it's not something we can figure out tonight."

"Because the ghosts can't leave the theatre, and it's closed for the evening, so you can't get in." Laurie nodded, seeing my predicament.

"Not to mention that the theatre's closed tomorrow for Thanksgiving," Ripley added.

"I hate to say it, but I actually think we might be at the end of our usefulness on this case."

Laurie frowned. "What are you thinking?"

"That maybe it's time to hand this off to Detective Anthony." I squared my posture.

Running his hand along his stubbly chin, Laurie inclined his head in agreement.

"And, given what a workaholic the woman is, she might even be there tomorrow," Ripley suggested.

I let my eyebrows raise. "Ah, good point. Ripley says Amaya might be there tomorrow," I told Laurie.

"She probably will, but I've got to be at my parents' place pretty early."

"Good," Ripley scoffed. "Less chance of Amaya getting distracted while she gazes at Laurie."

"That's okay." I patted his knee as I chuckled at Ripley's comment. "It's probably better if you don't come with. Detective Anthony might be more ... focused if it's just me."

His head jerked back. "What's that supposed to mean?"

I cocked an eyebrow at the man. "Laurence Peabody Turner, do *not* tell me you haven't noticed how the good detective drools over you."

"You don't know my middle name, do you?" he deadpanned.

"I do not." I lifted my chin.

His mouth quirked up in the corner. "It's Aaron, by the way. After my grandfather." Exhaling, he added, "Okay, well, I guess you don't need me tomorrow, then." The disappointment in his tone was palpable.

I moved a hand to cup his cheek. "It's the curse of being so handsome. Sometimes you have to sit things out."

"You two are getting sappy again." Ripley folded her arms. "I'm out of here."

Once she vanished, I leaned forward and kissed Laurie. He pulled back, cutting his eyes to the place Ripley had been standing.

"We probably shouldn't in front of—"

"She just left," I said, pressing my lips against his again.

He smiled. "In that case." Laurie pulled me closer. "I don't know if I'll ever get used to this," he whispered.

"The ghosts or the kissing?" I asked with an exhaled laugh.

He ran his thumb down my cheek. "Oh, the ghosts are no problem. The fact that you're mine? That's what I can't get over."

Placing his hands on my hips, Laurie pulled me into his lap.

❀

Laurie and I took Leo on a long walk through the sleepy city the next morning so I could see him before he had to go to his parents. We stopped by the store to grab the ingredients I needed as well as the cans of cranberry sauce since I hadn't followed my plan to leave the theatre early yesterday.

Once I got back to the Morrisey, I started on the stuffing, knowing I could always stick it back in the oven later. I didn't want to leave it for the last minute just in case my trip to see Detective Anthony took longer than I expected.

It was just after ten when Ripley and I made our way to the police headquarters building. Detective Anthony wasn't the only one working on the holiday, but the place was decidedly less busy than usual.

She eyed me warily as she called me to follow her back to her desk once the officer in reception notified her of my presence.

"So, what's up?" Detective Anthony leaned her forearms on her desk and threaded her fingers together.

I thought through the wording I'd carefully practiced with Ripley. Just because Laurie knew about my ghostly abilities now, didn't mean I could go telling everyone, especially not the rational detective sitting across from me.

"I know Winnie was less than helpful when you asked her who might've sent those poisoned chocolates to her the other day," I began. "But I've been working at the Third Avenue Theatre for the past few days, and I have cause to believe it's someone there."

Detective Anthony's eyes narrowed on me. "You just *happened* to get a job at the same place Winnie works during the week she was sent those chocolates?"

"I'm an artist. They needed someone to paint scenes and props." I lifted my shoulder with an indifference that was 100 percent fake.

The detective coughed out a laugh. "Okay, Meg. Go on. Who do you think sent them to Winnie?"

My gaze settled on Ripley who was looking over the file on the detective's desk. We'd decided that, as a backup plan, Ripley would look through the information the detective had compiled on the case while I talked to her. That way, if Detective Anthony didn't believe me or felt our evidence wasn't enough to look into, we could continue by ourselves, hopefully with a little more information than before.

Refocusing on Detective Anthony, I told her about what I'd learned at the theatre. "Well, through the people I've gotten to know at the theatre, I learned that Winnie sent one of the actors a box of chocolates she'd tampered with a few years back. Those chocolates had laxatives instead of fentanyl in them, but still. I think this could be a callback to that incident. It doesn't hurt that the person in question has new motivation to get Winnie out of the way."

"And what's that?"

"Winnie was apparently blackmailing the person's mother." Reading Detective Anthony's dubious expression, I quickly added, "I know it all sounds very dramatic, but things are toxic at that theatre. I don't know if you heard, but a woman was killed when a light dropped on her head the other day."

"I was briefed on the incident." The detective cleared her throat. "Forensics is looking into it. They're just swamped right now."

"I have cause to believe that this person might've killed Francine to further hurt Winnie. Winnie was fired after the incident since she's in charge of the lighting. I'm not sure if getting her fired was their endgame, but if they failed to kill Winnie once, they might try again."

"I asked your neighbor if she wanted us to look into this, and she was adamant that she wasn't worried about it." Detective Anthony sat back in her chair.

After a moment, however, she rummaged through her right-hand drawer of files. She pulled out one I'm assuming was connected to the chocolate case and flipped it open, ripping a fresh sheet of paper from the notebook next to her.

"She doesn't seem to be buying it, Megs. And I'm not seeing anything new here," Ripley said, frustration coating her words. "Should we do splash-and-search?" Her eyes moved to the water cooler in the corner.

The last time we'd wanted to get the detective away from her desk so I could look at the information we needed, Ripley had used her ghostly energy to knock over the cooler, creating a terrible mess.

Shaking my head as quickly as I could, I sent Ripley a pleading look. I didn't want Amaya to have to mop up a gallon or more of water on Thanksgiving. I could get the detective to search the earlier files.

"Would you mind checking something for me?" I asked. "I remember there being a sticker on the card that came with the poisoned chocolates, and I think I saw one just like it at the theatre, but I couldn't be sure," I lied, knowing the sticker was burned into my memory.

The detective flipped through her file to the first few pages. Ripley hung over her shoulder, scanning each paper as she went.

"It was a frog in cowboy boots," Detective Anthony answered, her lips twitching at the ridiculous sentence. "Was that what you saw at the theatre?"

"Exactly, and it was in the dressing room of the person Winnie sent the chocolates to before, another reason it could be her."

The detective seemed to count that as important because she jotted down a note for herself. "What's this person's name?" she asked.

"Yasmine Zara. Her mother is Petra Klein, the person who owns the Third Avenue. And Damien"—I wrinkled my nose—"I don't know his last name, actually, but Damien works there as well. I think he might be involved too."

"I'll look into this. Thank you, Meg." The detective straightened the pages inside the folder, but before she could close it, Ripley's eyes went wide.

"Oh, that's interesting," Ripley murmured.

I couldn't say anything, so I waited for Ripley to continue.

Her eyes flashed up to meet mine. "Remember when Winnie called in to the Morrisey meeting?"

I touched my earlobe, our sign for yes when I couldn't speak to her.

"And she said she was at work, but the internet wasn't strong enough for her to have the video on?" Ripley continued. She didn't wait for me to touch my ear again before adding, "Well, Amaya wrote *lied* next to Winnie's statement, and there's paperwork from another officer who was called to remove her from—"

Detective Anthony shut the folder and interrupted Ripley by saying, "Well, unless there's anything more..."

"Right." I stood, hoping Ripley had enough information for us to leave. "Thank you for listening."

The detective ducked her head. "Happy Thanksgiving, Meg."

"You, too, Detective." I sent her a weak smile as I walked out of the headquarters building. I filled my lungs with fresh air as I stepped out onto Fifth Avenue.

"So? Where was Winnie that day?" I asked Ripley, who was squinting toward the stadiums.

"A bank. My old bank, actually." She motioned to her left, which could've meant across the street or fifteen blocks down. I couldn't tell.

"Why was she at a bank?"

"I don't know. I couldn't read enough of the report before she closed it."

"Should we try to get back inside?" I asked, swallowing a groan at the thought of coming up with a believable reason we needed to talk to the detective yet again.

"Actually, no." Ripley's lips eased into a sly smirk. "I think we should go to the bank instead."

"It's Thanksgiving. It'll be closed."

"That's okay. I can go in for us." She mimed buffing her nails on her oversized flannel shirt.

"You really think this is important?" I asked, already tired.

Ripley nodded once. "I do. What if this gives us a different clue about who could've sent those chocolates?"

"But I thought we were sure it's Yasmine, or Damien."

"Then Amaya's already going to look into them. But maybe we'll learn something new at the bank that will confirm or deny that suspicion."

"The bank might not keep records of everyone they have

to kick out, and even if they do, we don't know where to look. Whereas we know where the information is inside there." I gestured back to the headquarters building.

Ripley huffed. "Megs, it was always going to be about spirits. There's no way anyone at a bank is going to give you information about their customers or why they were there."

She had a point. I'd been so excited to hand the case off to the detective, to truly be rid of it. Alas, it seemed things were never that easy.

"Okay, I'll come with you." I pouted. "Let's hope looking into why Winnie was at this bank, and why she lied about it, will help us close this case once and for all."

Twenty-One

The streets were fairly empty since most of the city was either cozy inside or traveling to be with family. Cozy inside was where I should've been. Instead, I was walking toward a closed bank in the frosty November temperatures. It was a good thing I'd already made the stuffing. At least I wasn't worried about my contribution to Thanksgiving dinner.

"If I can't even go inside with you, why do I need to be here? Can't I just go home and wait for you there?" I rubbed my hands up and down my arms, glancing longingly back toward the Morrisey.

"What if I have questions for you or if I want the ghosts to come outside and talk to you?" she said with a decisive shake of her head. "No, I think it's best if you come with."

I grumbled but acquiesced. Before too long, we arrived at the bank.

"Okay, you stay out here," Ripley said with a smirk, knowing I couldn't go inside even if I wanted to.

Immediately bored and cold, I took out my phone to keep myself busy while I waited. There was a text from Zoe wishing me a happy Thanksgiving. Smiling, I wrote back.

> Happy Thanksgiving to you too. How's the family getaway going?

Zoe must've been by her phone because she responded right away.

> It's amazing. Beautiful. The place is huge. We each have our own room. And the Stimacs have been really nice. I'm glad I gave them a chance. Thank you for the encouragement to do so.

My friend's gratitude warmed me for a moment. I was so glad she'd found a family after losing her mom to cancer. And while the Morrisey was quickly becoming a second family to her as well, the Stimacs had made a real effort to make Zoe feel included.

> I'm so glad you're having fun!

> Yes, and they're totally normal. Don't worry, only board games, hikes, and some flag football. Lol.

Before she left, Zoe had confided in me that she was worried about what she would find out about her new family on the upcoming trip. "Any family rich enough to have a mountain cabin seems like they might wear robes and be part of some weird secret society, or hunt people. I don't know," she'd said with a shiver.

> Glad there's been zero human hunting.

I added a winking emoji.

> They do have a weird obsession with pumpkin pies. There are at least five different kinds. But I think that's tame in the grand scheme of things.

> Totally tame. But ... you definitely have to try all of them and tell me which one is best.

> Oh, of course. Hope you and the Morrisey folks have a good day too.

> We will. I'll tell everyone you said hello.

My fingers hovered over the keyboard, wondering if I should fill her in about everything that had gone down in her absence. It wasn't as if she was particularly close to Julian or Winnie, and I didn't want to burden her with the issues we were having back home while she was trying to relax with the Stimacs. Also, Ripley chose that moment to emerge from the bank.

"Did you learn something?" I stood up, moving my phone to my ear so anyone passing by would just think I was on the phone.

"I did." Her eyes flashed with delight. "But I figured I'd let Scooter be the one to tell you."

"Scoo—" was all I got out before a second spirit appeared in front of me.

He looked to be from at least fifty years in the past. He had shaggy brown hair, blue eyes, and he wore coveralls that would've made it look like he'd been a painter if he wasn't also incredibly dirty. Even as a spirit, dirt seemed to cloud off the man like he was some kind of real-life Pig Pen character.

"Why are you so dusty?" I asked, curling my fingers to quell the urge to brush the dirt off his ghostly shoulders.

"Oh, I was a digger," he said, unfazed. "I was always underground. I guess it came with me in the afterlife."

"Digger?" I glanced back at the bank. "What does that mean?"

He widened his eyes and cocked his head as if it should be obvious.

I pulled in air sharply. "You dug under the bank?"

Touching his nose, he said, "Bingo, girlie."

I didn't love his use of *girlie* but kept focused on the questions piling up. I pointed to the building. "So, you robbed this bank, back in the day?"

"I would say that *attempted* is the better word for it." He coughed. "I didn't quite make it, you see. Ran out of air." A grimace painted his features.

Ripley adopted a similar expression. "Your bones are still under the bank?"

His chin plunged toward his chest in confirmation as he sucked his teeth in disappointment.

"But you know what Winnie was doing here on Saturday? Why she was removed by the police?" I asked.

His downcast expression morphed into one of intrigue. "Ah, scarf lady. Yes, I do."

"That's why I chose him to talk to you," Ripley interjected. "Of all the ghosts in there, he's definitely the most gossipy."

Scooter didn't seem to take offense to that label. In fact, he placed a hand on his chest and bowed forward. "Thank you, Ripley." Counting on his fingers, he said, "Yes, five days ago, a woman like you described, with scarves flowing every which way, came in to talk to one of the tellers. It was a rather slow day, and close to the end of business hours since it was a Saturday and they leave early on those days. But even though there wasn't a lineup behind her, Francine began to get irritated that the woman wouldn't leave; that's what caught my attention."

"Francine? Wait. Francine worked here? Our Francine from the theatre?" I looked to Ripley, whose eyes lit up with excitement.

"Based on what Ripley told me, yes, it's the same Francine," Scooter explained.

"And you heard what Winnie was asking Francine?" I sat on the nearby bench, motioning for him to sit next to me.

He did, looking as if he was grateful to take a seat, even though he didn't have a physical body any longer. "Yes, when I went over to Francine's till, the woman with the scarves was asking for Francine to buy her more time."

Ripley and I shared a look.

"More time?" I asked.

"To which Francine responded that she was a teller and that she didn't have anything to do with loan repayments. This Winnie character said that Francine could at least *ask* someone if it would be possible. She said she was working on getting the money, but it was going to be a few more weeks."

I frowned. "Winnie's behind on her loans?"

"That's what it sounds like." Ripley worried her lip.

"Then Francine asked Winnie why she should bother helping her," Scooter told us. "She said Winnie took her job and rubbed it in her face every time she came in to make a deposit. She didn't care if her investor friend lost her money."

"An investor friend?" Ripley asked, having obviously not heard that part of the story inside the bank. "Did she mention who?"

"Nope. She just gave this woe-is-me kind of speech about how he was a guy from her building and she thought she could trust him, but he'd made some poor decisions, and now, not only did it change her plans, but she was going to be late on her credit card payments until she figured out a solution."

Again, Ripley and I caught each other's eyes. My grim emotions were mirrored in my friend's expression.

A guy in her building.

"Julian," Ripley whispered.

"So that's why he was stealing things from the other residents." I realized. "He must've been stealing and reselling. That's why certain pieces weren't there. He'd sold off the more expensive stuff."

"And kept the not valuable stuff like Darius's socks," Ripley deadpanned.

Scooter squinted one eye. "I don't know who Darius is, but when Francine asked whether the guy could try to reinvest the money to see if he might make it back, Winnie said that wouldn't be possible, that he'd quit and had moved on to much-less-savory means of making ends meet. She said she was going to have to take matters into her own hands if she wanted revenge. That was when Francine called the cops to remove her from the building."

"Revenge? Less-savory means?" My flesh seemed to tighten with alarm as I looked at Ripley. "Winnie knew Julian was the one who was stealing the packages?"

Ripley adopted a haunted look. "What if she *meant* for him to steal those chocolates from her? What if the reason Winnie won't talk to us is because she's never actually been in danger because she's the one behind it all?"

Twenty-Two

Walking back to the Morrisey after we'd thanked Scooter for his help, it felt like *I* was the ghost. Or maybe more of a zombie.

Ripley and I barely spoke. Did I even blink? I floated through the sparse groupings of pedestrians, thinning even more as the clock passed twelve noon and people began to leave for their Thanksgiving plans.

Winding up the stairwell to my apartment, the aroma of Thanksgiving meals poured out from the apartments of my neighbors. It should've made me feel excited about our upcoming meal. Instead, I couldn't help but think how everything was a lie. It was all fake. My neighbors had been worried about Winnie. They'd wanted to help keep her safe.

But she hadn't needed our help at all.

Was that why she'd shut down Detective Anthony, and why she'd told me not to bother? Had she steered me away from Francine because she was the only one who knew the truth about Winnie and Julian? Had Winnie dropped that light on her head before I could talk to her?

The thought made me sick.

I hated suspecting one of my neighbors like that, but I'd been wrong about what people were capable of before, especially when they'd lost a lot of money and felt like there were no other options. I wouldn't make the mistake of underestimating Winnie like I had with Quentin. Also, as much as I'd felt like I knew Quentin, I knew practically nothing about Winnie. She shared so little with us that maybe I should've jumped to this conclusion much earlier in the process.

Back in my apartment, I blurted out all my worries and theories to Ripley, who'd apparently been going through the same thoughts in her mind while we'd been walking, because she nodded and winced as I mentioned each terrible wonderment.

"Regular Winnie might not have done any of it, but we both felt how the theatre ghosts affected us." I shook my head sadly. "We know exactly how much worse it made our thoughts and impulses."

"Do you think we should go back to the police?" Ripley asked. "Should we tell the detective?"

I turned on the oven so it would be ready for the stuffing. "I'd bet even our workaholic detective is gone at this point. It can wait until tomorrow. What do I do if she comes to dinner, though? How do I pretend I don't suspect it could've been her?"

"Maybe you shouldn't go," Ripley said. "Maybe drop off the stuffing and tell them you're not feeling well. That way you don't have to face her if she does come."

I liked the idea that I might have options. I could see how I felt once I got there.

I lost myself in reheating the stuffing, the calming scents of thyme, sage, and rosemary settling my nerves a little as the dish warmed in the oven, browning and crisping up along the edges. Once two o'clock rolled around, I was resigned to go. I wouldn't let Winnie ruin one of my favorite holidays with my Morrisey family. Plus, Nancy said Winnie wasn't going to come. She probably wouldn't even be there.

By the time I made my way down to the lobby, carrying the warm dish of stuffing with oven mitt-covered hands, a bag holding the canned cranberry sauce, and a can opener hanging off my left arm, the big table had been set. A quick scan of the lobby proved to me that Winnie wasn't there, and I relaxed.

"Nutmeg, that looks delicious," Nancy said as I took off the foil covering.

Beaming, I gestured to the turkey she'd already carved and plated on three different platters spanning the length of the table. "So does the turkey."

She brushed off my compliment. "Baking is baking, whether it's turkey or rolls." She shrugged even though her statement went against everything I'd ever heard about the difficulty of baking a turkey.

We moved on to discussing the cranberry-orange muffins she'd brought. They looked amazing too. The multiple trial bakes she'd done had definitely paid off.

A few more neighbors joined, filling out the rest of the menu as they set their dishes on the table and claimed their spots. Just as Nancy called us to sit down, Art turned on some music. We were all taking our seats when I squinted one eye and turned my attention to Art on the other side of the table.

"Is this song about mashed potatoes?" I asked with a giggle.

Art stuck out his chest proudly. "Why, yes, it is. Thank you for noticing, Nutmeg. You'd be surprised at how many songs there are out there about Thanksgiving foods. I put together a whole playlist."

We all laughed as the song continued to wax poetic about the different qualities of potatoes. The next one was titled "My Sweet Potato." We suppressed our laughter as we went around the table, telling each other the thing we were most thankful for this year, per Nancy's request.

There were many smiles as my neighbors explained how thankful they were for new jobs, steady jobs, family and friends, changes, dreams realized, and much more.

When it was my turn, I told them I was most thankful for moving back to the Morrisey, because they were truly my family, and I would always love living here, especially since it brought back my artistic confidence. I think I saw Nancy wipe away a tear after that.

Then we dug in. The food was amazing, and the songs about potatoes kept on coming. Ripley floated around the table, catching bits and pieces of the different conversations going on during the meal. It was wonderful, and I realized how much I'd missed the Morrisey in my years on the East Coast.

But despite the warm, lovely feelings swirling through the lobby as we ate, my spine stiffened. Gazing out at my

Morrisey family, the overwhelming feeling I experienced was guilt. The realization felt like a strike to the gut. Winnie was one of us. Just because we'd all been wrong about Quentin didn't mean I needed to look at all my neighbors as murderers.

There had to be an explanation for what happened to Francine, and why Winnie lied about being at the bank that Saturday instead of at work. The mere fact that she'd opted not to show up at her favorite holiday of the year told me something big was going on with the woman.

When I'd eaten my fill and officially couldn't stand to listen to one more song about potatoes, mashed or otherwise, I told Nancy that I was going to make a plate for Winnie and take it up to her.

"I feel bad she didn't want to come," I said.

Nancy smiled as she patted my cheek. "Such a caring soul, our Nutmeg. Sure, doll. Let me know if you need help carrying anything."

I told her I could manage, and that I'd come back for my stuffing dish later, before pointing myself in the direction of the stairwell. Ripley walked next to me as I climbed the stairs to the fourth floor.

"Meg, are you sure about this?"

"It's Winnie." I pushed my way into the fourth-floor hallway.

The apprehension didn't disappear from Ripley's expression, but she also didn't stop me as I stepped up to apartment 4E.

Balancing the plate of food in one hand, I jammed my finger down onto Winnie's buzzer and waited.

Nothing. No sounds of a television or music coming from inside. It was eerily quiet.

Fear spiked in my chest, making it hard to breathe. I shot a panicked glance at Ripley.

What if the chocolate poisoner had come back to finish the job? My guilt increased tenfold. Here I'd been considering her as the prime suspect and she could be in danger.

I pressed the buzzer three more times in quick succession.

"Okay, okay." Winnie's voice spilled through the door as her footsteps stomped toward me. An angry Winnie swung the door toward herself and scowled out at me. "I don't know what you're playing at, Meg Dawson, but I'm really not in the mood—"

But in my absolute relief that she was unharmed, I cut her off. "Oh, good. I'm so glad you're okay, Winnie. I got worried when you didn't show up at dinner, so I brought you a plate." I shoved it toward her, using the forward motion to get my foot over the threshold of her apartment. If I could gain Ripley access, we might not have to be in the dark about everything anymore.

Winnie took the plate, stepping back in surprise. Seeing my opening, I realized I might be able to do even better than gaining Ripley access. Acting as if Winnie had invited me in, I entered the apartment, Ripley ahead of me. Winnie might've answered the buzzer, but I wanted to make sure there wasn't anyone in the place holding her hostage or anything. Ripley seemed to have the same idea because she checked in the bedroom and the bathroom while I scanned the living room and kitchen.

The door shut behind us as Ripley gave a thumbs-up,

telling me it was all clear. A small smile overtook the bewilderment previously encompassing her expression.

"You didn't have to do this," Winnie whispered at the plate, as if it might've brought itself up the stairs. But then her eyes met mine and I saw the gratitude there. "I was getting hungry. I just felt so embarrassed."

"Why?" I asked, frowning at my neighbor.

"Um … Meg?" Ripley's voice quavered slightly, but I couldn't look away from Winnie, whose chin bunched up like she might break into sobs.

Winnie shook her head, placing the plate of food on the counter in her kitchen. "I put so much into that theatre, so many years. I thought it would be where I worked forever, where I ended my career. And now look at me. Jobless. And that's only half of it." She raised her hands, then let them fall by her sides.

"I don't know what happened between you and Petra, but could you ask her for a second chance?" I stepped toward Winnie. "Carter can't have the authority to fire you for good, can he?"

She sniffed. "I made a mistake with Petra. It was stupid, and … no, I'm not sure I can ask a favor of her after what I pulled."

Intrigue burned in my chest. The blackmail. "What did you do?"

Her eyes met mine, but she quickly turned away. "It was that place. It gave me ideas I never would've thought of before. I swear it's cursed like everyone says."

I couldn't argue with her about that. "Right. So, go apologize. Whatever you did to Petra, whatever you said, you can ask for forgiveness."

"You don't understand. I crossed a line." There was a wildness in Winnie's eyes that made me stop and take a step back.

"Meg, you need to see this." Ripley's tone was icy.

Tearing my attention from Winnie, I looked back toward my ghostly best friend. Her spirit was rigid as she repeatedly jabbed a finger toward the wall behind Winnie's dining table. I coughed, feeling as if a ball of sawdust had formed in my throat.

On the wall hung a large painting of a cow lounging on a couch.

"Cowch," Ripley croaked out, her eyes widening with fear.

Turning back toward Winnie, I didn't need to point as Ripley had done. Winnie already saw what had caught my attention. She worried her lip between her teeth.

"Winnie? I thought you said Julian had stolen that painting from you." My voice was the only steady part of me as my neighbor cringed in response.

She nodded only once. "He did."

A chill ran over my skin. "So, why is it hanging in your apartment?"

Winnie's expression was that of a trapped woman, but as I glanced at the door she'd closed behind me, I realized I was the one who'd walked right into a trap.

Twenty-Three

Facts hit me in the face one by one as the reality of my situation sank in.

Winnie had known about Julian stealing. She must've somehow found out he was selling her beloved painting and had decided to get even with him, using the chocolates.

In short, my first thoughts about Winnie had been right —before Thanksgiving with my neighbors had caused me to go all soft and sentimental.

"I can block her if you want to run." Ripley was already sidling toward the door.

But this wasn't Quentin, who had been bigger than me and who'd easily physically overpowered me. Winnie was shorter, and she didn't strike me as particularly buff—though I couldn't quite tell her true body type under all those scarves and flowing layers, and I *had* seen her kick the stairwell door once with impressive force to keep it open. But this was a woman who'd poisoned and used lights dropping from ceilings to get her revenge, if my terrible suspicions were correct. She hadn't stabbed anyone because she wasn't strong enough.

And I was going to get some answers.

"You knew. Didn't you?" I shoved the question toward Winnie much like I had with the plate of food.

She let out a nervous laugh. "Knew what?"

Gritting my teeth, I steadied myself before saying, "Don't act ignorant, Winnie. I know everything. I know you've used chocolates as a punishment before. I know Julian lost a bunch of your savings. I even know that you were mad enough at Francine for not helping you extend your loan payments to get revenge on her. I don't care if it's Thanksgiving, I want you to come with me to the police station and tell them what you did."

"I will go no such place with you, young woman," Winnie said, glaring at me. "Why would I want to hurt Francine? She was my friend."

Now it was my turn to glare. "Some friend you were to her. Do you make it a point to steal jobs from all your friends?"

"I didn't steal her job." Winnie's expression softened. "Though, I can see how it might look like that. Petra and I made the decision to switch her to the concessions stand and ticket booth for her own good."

"You and Petra?" I blinked.

"Francine and Carter were fighting every day," Winnie explained. "Francine wasn't very good at the lighting. Petra wanted to help her get out of the theatre. She didn't think it was a good place for her. Petra's always trying to look out for people's best interests like that. She sure does love an underdog."

Hearing Winnie talk so complimentary of the woman I thought she hated, the woman she was blackmailing, affected my balance, and I reached for the wall to steady myself.

"Petra knew if Francine made less money at the ticket stand, she'd have to get a second job. Once she did, once she had a foot out the door, we were constantly trying to convince her to go full time at the bank."

"But you went there trying to get her to help you with your loans." I frowned.

Winnie discharged a grunted breath. "Not one of my best days. Wait. How'd you know about that?" Her eyes narrowed at me.

"Francine told me," I lied, feeling terrible about using the dead woman as cover for my ghostly secret, but that wasn't what was important right now. The most critical thing now was catching Winnie. "But you lied to the police, to all of us at that meeting, about where you were."

Recoiling slightly, Winnie said, "As I said, not one of my better days. Nancy called that meeting, and I was too embarrassed to admit that I'd let Julian squander a good portion of my savings. I lied. You never know who banks where. It's a small community. I wasn't sure if one of the Morrisey folks would recognize that bank and do some digging if they saw it in the background."

The fact that it had been Ripley's bank made it difficult to argue with her logic there.

"And once I told you all about being at work, I had to continue that when I spoke to the police."

"So, you didn't hate Francine?" I tried to catch up. "You wanted her to work at the bank?"

"Yes. It was a much steadier job and a better environment. She was drowning in the complaints of Carter and the rest of the crew at the Third Avenue."

Blinking at Ripley, I said, "If it was so bad, why did you stay?"

"I thought I could change it. I was hoping to buy the theatre from Petra. That's why I had Julian investing my money. I had a good amount of savings and wanted to see if I could double it, like he promised me he could." She rolled her eyes. "I should've known better."

This wasn't panning out like I thought it would. Her explanation was leaving me feeling unsteady on my feet. For stability, I grasped on to the most damning piece of evidence I had against Winnie.

"What about the chocolates you sent to Yasmine? How am I supposed to trust that you didn't try the same thing with Julian to teach him a lesson when you found out he was stealing?" I motioned toward the painting. "You obviously knew he was pawning the stuff he stole from people's doorsteps."

"Hold on." Winnie held up her hands and stepped forward. "I didn't get this back until two days ago, *after* Julian ate those chocolates. And, as for the chocolates, the ones I sent to Yasmine just made her need to use the bathroom. I didn't try to kill anyone." She placed a hand on her chest as if she was offended I would even think that. "Like I said, that theatre is cursed. It makes people mad."

Narrowing my eyes, I said, "Like how it made you take

things too far with Petra? What did you do? Why does everyone think you tried to blackmail her?"

My mind was whirring with the new information I was getting. If we were back to it not being Winnie, it had to be Yasmine or Damien trying to protect Petra. Which meant that I needed to figure out what Winnie had fought with Petra about.

"I-I was desperate; you have to understand that," Winnie said, her eyes wild again. "I'd recently found out about the money I'd lost, and I felt my dream of buying the theatre slipping away from me. Petra's rich. She doesn't need the money. I tried to convince her to let me buy a portion of it from her or rent to own, but she wouldn't budge. She told me she had another offer. I snapped. I threatened her with blackmail."

"Imogen was right," Ripley said, a breathy quality to her tone.

"What did you have to blackmail her with?" I asked, needing the missing piece, the information Imogen hadn't known and neither had any of the theatre ghosts. Had it been contained in that purple folder after all?

"It was Damien," Winnie admitted with a huff. "I learned that he got arrested for assault about a month ago. Joe, a friend of mine, works at a bar down by the stadiums. He said there was a big brawl centered around some football game. A guy was running his mouth about the Seattle team, like he was asking for a fight. A group of guys tried to get him to leave, but he came at them. Damien jumped in to help when it was clear the guys were no match for the instigator. Joe recognized Damien from the times we'd all gone there to celebrate after a show, and wanted to make sure he was all right since it got pretty out of hand. When I called the station to find out if Damien needed help, they said he'd already been released, that the charges had been dropped. I figured Petra had pulled some strings, something I was sure her holier-than-thou friends at the charity wouldn't find becoming, especially not of someone they were considering for a position on the board of their charity."

"They really would've kicked her out for helping Damien?"

Winnie nodded somberly. "They're all about using their status for good, not for personal gain, which is how they would've seen her bribing someone to get them to drop the charges against Damien. But when I confronted her about Damien's arrest, I could tell right away that Petra had no idea that it'd happened. I'm not sure what was worse: seeing her realize that Damien had lied to her or her comprehending that I was trying to use her love for Damien against her. I was disgusted with myself." A sheepishness came over her. "Despite that, in my desperation, once I learned that it was the lights that had killed Francine, I thought I could blame the poor maintenance on Damien since he was the one who checked them for me. The thought made me realize I was out of control, and I left. I let Carter fire me."

"Do you think the chocolates could've been from Damien? To get you back for threatening to blackmail Petra, even if it was fake?" I asked. "I mean, you said it yourself that he was probably the one to blame for the light falling on Francine."

"I said nothing of the sort." Winnie's brittle exterior softened as she noticed I didn't understand. "The heights scare me, so Damien checks the lights for me out of the goodness of his heart. Which is all the more reason for me to feel awful for using him the way that I did against Petra, for even entertaining the idea that he should take the fall for Francine's death."

"What about Yasmine?" I asked, uncomfortably aware that I was grasping at that point.

Winnie jerked her head in the negative. "That girl's going places. She sticks with the Third Avenue because of her mother, but once Petra lets go of that place, Yasmine will be getting the lead in shows all over the country if she wants. She wouldn't risk any of that to try to get me out of the way."

"Ask her about the purple folder," Ripley reminded me.

Right. "There was a purple folder on your desk in the light booth. I saw it later in Yasmine's dressing room. I thought it might be linked to the blackmail, but..." I didn't know how to finish the statement, so I didn't.

"Oh, that?" Winnie's cheeks grew red. "No, the purple folder is between me and Yasmine."

I glared at her, telling her this was not the time for more secrets.

She cleared her throat. "Yasmine uses that to give me notes on how she feels her levels are during the rehearsal each day. We pass it back and forth, and I adjust for the next rehearsal."

"I thought you said you turned Yasmine down all the time because she was too pitchy?" Ripley asked Winnie, as if the woman could hear her.

I repeated the question to Winnie.

"Well, yes. I *used* to do that. But when I started considering buying the theatre, I figured having Yasmine on my good side couldn't hurt. I also knew that if I started asking all the actors what they wanted when it came to the sound levels, it would be a nightmare, so the folder was how we got around that, in secret."

"So, you really have no idea who sent you those chocolates?" I asked, deflating.

"I don't. Especially now that I've got some space from the theatre, I'm realizing nothing we fought about was all that bad." She picked up the plate of food. "Now that you're done accusing me of murder, do you mind if I eat this?"

Everything felt heavy. Winnie sat down at the table. She gestured for me to sit. I slumped into a chair next to her.

"I'm sorry I wasn't more helpful or open. I was embarrassed." Winnie poked her fork at a sweet potato and popped it in her mouth. "I appreciate you trying to keep me safe, though."

Mumbling something that I hoped was close to *you're welcome,* I busied myself with looking around the room. The cow painting caught my eye, reminding me of the final question I had about Winnie Wisteria as she pertained to this whole mess.

"How'd you get this painting back, then?" I asked, standing to inspect the piece.

Winnie finished chewing her most recent bite and swallowed. "Ah, Carter found it for me, actually. He heard me telling Francine about how I'd bought it, and then again, when it was stolen. He said he found it in a pawnshop, of all places."

A Poisoned Package

"Most pawnshops I know of don't take art," Ripley muttered as she wandered around the apartment, bored. "Too hard for them to resell. Especially something like that."

Searching for something to say about the odd thing, I said, "It is definitely well-made." I tilted the painting toward me, checking out the back of the canvas. "If the artist stretches her own canvas, she's very good at it."

But before I could set it back, flush with the wall once more, I noticed something odd. The back of the canvas had diagonal pieces of wood acting as supports in each of the four corners. That wasn't unusual with a piece this large. What was odd was that there was a section of fabric stapled over the corner closest to me. The fabric was cream colored and might've blended in with the canvas that had been curled around the frame, but I could see the difference. I also knew there was no reason for the corner of a painting to be covered.

"This is odd." I craned my neck so I could get a better look. "Is covering the back corner in fabric a signature of the artist?" I glanced over at Winnie.

"She paints pictures of cows lounging on couches. She doesn't need an odd signature like that." Winnie set down her fork and got up to join me so she could see for herself.

Frowning, she grabbed a pair of scissors from a drawer in the kitchen and then returned, stabbing a hole into the triangle of material stapled to the back. Inside was a small device.

"Is that a microphone?" I asked, confusion creasing my forehead.

Winnie glowered at the thing before dropping it onto the

wood floor and stomping it with her shoe until it was only a small pile of wires and plastic. "That liar. I knew it was him."

Cocking my head, and trying to catch up, I asked, "Wait. Who?"

"Carter," Winnie answered in exasperation, as if I should've known. "He said he brought me the painting as a peace offering, to say he was sorry for having to let me go from the theatre, but it was all just a way to listen in, to spy on me."

Ripley scoffed. "Ah-ha! That must be why Carter always had his earbuds in. He wasn't listening to the musical numbers. He was spying on Winnie."

"Why would he want to spy on you?" I asked Winnie, following Ripley's logic.

My neighbor's conviction wavered. "Well, the artist didn't put it there. She's an eighty-five-year-old woman. What cause would she have to listen to me? Plus, I suspect that Carter was the other person interested in purchasing the theatre, the one Petra mentioned when she said she had another offer."

"Why would that mean he needed to listen to you?" I asked, still not catching up fully.

Her eyes went wide. "I don't know, but I'd bet anything he's lost money with Julian as well."

The apartment, that cow, it all seemed to tilt around me. "What makes you say that?"

Winnie's chest expanded with a revelatory inhale. "When I was talking to Francine one day, I told her about my plan to have Julian invest my savings so I could finally buy the theatre. Carter walked by and said he was looking for someone to help with his investments, too, and could he get Julian's contact information. After I gave it to him, Francine said I shouldn't have because she thought he wanted to buy the place, and I shouldn't give myself competition by helping him get more money." Winnie scoffed, "I thought she was being paranoid, but I guess she knew more than I gave her credit for."

Glancing over at Ripley, remembering what she'd said about pawnshops not taking art, I came to a conclusion. "You said Carter knew about the painting getting stolen?"

Winnie confirmed that he did. "I needed something to break up a fight he and Francine were having, about him messing up the chocolate order for Petra. I told them about my cow being stolen, and Carter huffed off in a storm."

I grabbed her hand. "Winnie, if Carter knew about the painting, he might've figured out that it was Julian stealing stuff in our building way before we did. What if he sent those chocolates to you, knowing Julian was going to take them before you could get them?"

Despite the severity of what I was accusing the director of, Winnie simply gave a small hop of her shoulders. "It would've been a great plan, because if I got them first, he'd get me out of the way. If not, he'd hurt Julian. Win-win for him."

Gaze landing on the destroyed microphone on the floor, I knelt to pick up the pieces. "We have to tell the police."

Winnie swallowed and said, "Won't they all be at home, though?"

Frowning, I chewed on my lip. "Let me try Detective Anthony first." She didn't pick up, and I didn't know what to say in a message. "There must be someone at the headquarters building. Let's just go see who we can talk to."

"I'll go ahead and check if anyone's at the building," Ripley said, disappearing.

Winnie and I moved quickly, rushing through the lobby, blazing past the remaining Morrisey residents eating pie and bagging up leftovers, and up toward Fifth Avenue, hoping there was someone who could help us left at the station.

Twenty-Four

"How are you walking so fast?" Winnie complained a few steps behind me as I huffed up the inclined streets of Pioneer Square toward Fifth Avenue. She grappled with the silky scarves.

Normally, her flowing clothing made her look dramatic and effortless. As we rushed up the hill, her scarves looked like they were trying to strangle her.

As I approached Third Avenue, Ripley appeared in front of me. Glancing back, I saw that Winnie was still puffing after me, but probably far enough away that she wouldn't be able to hear me talk to Ripley.

"Anyone at the police station?" I whispered as Ripley fell in step beside me.

She dipped her chin. "A skeleton crew, but they're there."

"Perfect." I turned to see if Winnie had caught up to me by now. But as I checked behind me, my neighbor wasn't there. "Winnie?" I spun around.

She was gone.

It was then that I noticed the building we were passing by—the Third Avenue Theatre.

Anger boiled inside me. Had Winnie ducked inside the theatre to avoid talking to the police with me? She'd seemed willing to talk to them minutes ago, but the woman was slippery and more than secretive.

"Did she change her mind?" Ripley asked with a frown.

Groaning as I backtracked, I slipped down the alley behind the theatre.

"The question is, does she still have her keys?" I stopped in front of the back entrance and pulled on the handle, finding it unlocked.

"She didn't even lock it behind her?" Ripley snorted. "Amateur."

I pulled out my phone and turned on my flashlight as I crept forward into the pitch-black hallway.

"Winnie?" I called out. I meant to say her name at full volume, but it came out in a cracked whisper instead, as if my voice was worried about what might be lurking in the shadows.

In addition to being dark, the theatre was eerily quiet, especially when I was used to hearing sounds of rehearsal, instruments being tuned, and Carter screaming at everyone involved.

Thinking about Carter made my skin go clammy, and a sense of urgency rushed through me. We needed to get the police over to his house. I didn't care if it was Thanksgiving, the man had tried to kill Winnie and, based on whether he came out of that coma, might've succeeded with Julian. I moved down the hallway, hesitating at the crossroads that would either lead me to the stage or down another hallway.

Would Winnie have gone straight toward her booth, or somewhere else?

A distant clanging noise came from the stage, something that normally wouldn't be audible, but seemed amplified in the quiet.

I moved, bounding up the steps and onto the stage as I swept my light across the dark expanse.

Empty.

Someone cried out in pain. The sound seemed to come from everywhere at once as it echoed in the empty space.

"Maybe she didn't come in on her own after all," Ripley croaked.

"Winnie?" This time my voice shook. My fingers did too as I started to dial 9-1-1. Was Carter here? This place was big enough that I could hide until the police showed up.

"Put down the phone." His tone was as icy as it pierced through the silence. Just like the cry moments ago, Carter's voice seemed to surround me.

"I can't see him, Meg." Ripley rushed around, searching as quickly as she could.

I froze but didn't let go of my phone, trying to buy her some time to search.

Wherever Carter was, he saw my indecision, and anticipated my calculations.

"If you try anything, I push her off," he said cooly.

Pointing the flashlight up with a gasp, I found them. Carter had Winnie up on the catwalk with him. One hand encircled her throat, the other held her arms behind her back.

The two of them stood near one of the openings that led to the even smaller walkways Damien used to service the lights.

If Winnie fell from that height... I swallowed the bitter taste of terror that filled my mouth. Slowly, I set down my phone. I kept the flashlight facing up so I could see them.

"Good girl. Now step away." Carter's voice felt like an unwanted hand running fingertips along the backs of my arm. I couldn't see Ripley. I stepped away.

"Two more, for good measure," he added.

Winnie let out a strangled sound, then gagged as if Carter had tightened his grip around her neck.

"Stop, Meg!" Ripley's voice returned to my side, rushing back from wherever she'd disappeared to.

I pinwheeled my arms as I stopped and felt the lack of stage under my right foot. A burst of energy came from Ripley as she pushed me away from the opening.

Tottering back away from the hole I'd almost walked into, I found the trapdoor open, looming to my right. In the darkness, added to the black paint of the stage, I hadn't seen it. That must've been the clanging sound I'd heard. I'd bet Carter had pressed the button to open it after grabbing Winnie from the street, and it had just now clicked into place.

Slightly sketchy from the effort, Ripley sagged forward in relief. She scowled up at Carter, who tutted in disappointment. My heart hammered in my chest, and everything felt a little wobbly at the realization of what had almost happened.

"Ah, I suppose that would've been too easy," he said.

I shook off the encounter and deliberately squared my posture. "Find the others," I whispered to Ripley, who nodded and disappeared. Moments later, she reappeared by my side with Nathanial, Katherine, and Janet in tow. Four ghosts. I could work with this.

A smile peeled across my face, and I shot a haughty look at Carter.

"You won't get away with this." I stepped around the trapdoor, craning my neck so I could keep him in my sights.

He laughed, a cold sound that made my lungs constrict as if I'd just sucked in a freezing breath. "I already have," he said.

"Should we push him?" Janet asked, glancing up to the catwalk.

Ripley shook her head. "Winnie's too close to him. We can't be sure it wouldn't knock her off too."

Seeing that my ghostly friends needed time to run through the options, I decided I could do my part and keep Carter talking. "How do you figure you've *gotten away* with anything?" I asked, venom in my tone.

"Simple," he said. "I heard you confront Winnie about everything through that microphone before Winnie destroyed it. I figured you'd be headed to the police station, and I waited to intercept you so I could tell them *my* version of the story instead."

"Which is?" I gritted my teeth.

"That you figured out Winnie sent herself the chocolates, knowing Julian would eat them, then killed Francine with the light because she wouldn't help her with her money problems. You confronted her about it, and she lured you up here, only to push you off. Then, unable to live with what she'd done, she threw herself off the catwalk after you. So tragic." He tilted his head in consideration. "I think a note might be sufficient to fill in the blanks."

Winnie let out a strangled laugh. "I wouldn't write a note, you idiot."

"No," he said in that silky, calm voice of his. "But Miss Meg would. Such a diligent sleuth might've written down everything for the police, just to make sure she didn't leave out any details."

I hated that he was right. I *had* done that before.

The ghosts seem to have hit a dead end with ideas because Janet let out a frustrated groan next to me and said, "It's hopeless. There's nothing we can do."

"I think you need to run, Meg." Nathanial's tone was steady.

Katherine, for the first time in what I guessed to be a long time, agreed with them both. "Save yourself, Meg."

"How do you know we haven't already told the police?" I asked, trying not to let the theatre ghosts' defeat become mine. "Winnie destroyed your microphone. We could've asked them to meet us here instead of going to them."

Carter moved Winnie closer to the edge. He narrowed his eyes. "Don't play with me, kid," Carter growled. "If you really mean that, it only gives me more reason to make this quick." His grip tightened around Winnie's throat.

She wailed in response. "Meg, he's right. It's hopeless. You've got to save yourself. Run." The last word was barely a whisper as he clamped down even harder.

Hearing the words so recently spoken by the theatre ghosts repeated by Winnie made me stop. My gaze flashed to

Ripley. Our eyes locked as we understood the same thing simultaneously.

Their defeat was rubbing off on Winnie, just like their bad energy had before. Her body slumped as she gave in to what was happening to her. But ... if we could turn the tables and infuse her with enough confidence... Would that powerful kick I'd seen her use before on the stairwell door at the Morrisey be enough to get free of Carter's grip? I had to try.

"She won't leave you, Winnie," Carter said, confidence leaking from his words.

"Think positive thoughts," I whispered to the ghosts. Then I called up to Carter, "Okay, fine. Don't hurt her. I'll do what you ask."

"I knew you'd come to your senses," Carter crooned.

I glanced over at the ghosts, who were all staring at me with intense concentration as if they were trying to read my mind.

"Not like that," Ripley scoffed. "Say things aloud."

"Quick, say positive things," Janet circled her hands at her fellow ghosts. They started a barrage of "It'll be okay!" "You can do it!" and "You're strong, Winnie. You can fight him!"

"Come up here," Carter called to me, causing the ghosts to fall into silence.

"Don't, Meg. It's a trap." Ripley's ghostly hands grabbed at me as if they might be able to stop me from moving.

Carter noticed my wavering. "How about this? I'm going to count down from thirty. If you're not here by the time I get to one, I'm pushing her." He tilted his head as he watched me consider. "Thirty ... twenty-nine..."

My eyes met Ripley's wide ones for a split second. Before I could register the fear behind them, I ran.

Without my flashlight, it was almost impossible to see once I jumped down the staircase off the stage and raced into the dark hallway. My eyes adjusted quickly, and I wasn't completely in the dark thanks to the illuminated exit sign at the end of the hall. My feet pounded up the staircase, the sound almost as loud as my heart beating in my ears.

Lungs burning for more air, I spun around and ran down the upper hallway, toward the catwalk.

Carter's unfeeling voice still counted down the seconds. "Twenty ... nineteen..."

I moved faster than he and I had during our whirlwind tour during my first day.

"Five ... four... Ah, there she is."

My feet skidded to a stop at the edge of the catwalk. The light from my flashlight still pointed up, illuminating the two figures teetering over the middle of the stage. I panted, gulping in lungfuls of air as I tried to figure out what to do next.

"We need something even more empowering," Ripley urged the ghosts from the stage. "Nathanial, what about that uplifting song from *Newsies*?"

It was a good idea. And since the cast had just performed the musical before this one, I hoped the ghosts would know the words. They should. I wasn't in the cast of *Singing in the Rain*, but after a week of being around during rehearsals, I could sing most of the songs.

"Oh, good idea," Nathanial said. "'Seize the Day.'"

But instead of reciting lines, a gorgeous voice began to sing, "Now is the time to seize the day." It was Katherine. She paused, then added, "Stare down the odds and seize the day."

Janet and Nathanial's voices joined in: "Minute by minute. That's how you win it. We will find a way. But let us seize the day."

Ripley, who I'd watched the movie with before, tried her best to keep up with the different lyrics from the Broadway version. I turned my focus on Winnie.

My neighbor's brow furrowed as if she wasn't sure what was happening, but a light returned to her previously hopeless eyes.

The song was working.

As they moved farther into the opening, Nathanial began slapping his hands on his ghostly thighs to signify the drums in the background of the original song. I needed to give Winnie more time. If she had more hope, she might be able to struggle free.

"So, you knew Julian was stealing packages from our building?" I asked Carter as casually as I could.

Carter scoffed. "Not until I went to his place to confront him about all the money he lost me. The moment I shoved my way into that apartment of his, I saw the packages and that stupid cow painting Winnie had been going on about."

"Hey," she croaked out, seemingly just as hurt by that comment as she had been by his hand wrapped around her throat.

I gave her a warning glare. In the background, the ghosts

were repeating the refrain. My heart lifted at the lines of the song while Carter continued.

"I put it together quite quickly after that, and I convinced him to give me the painting just in case I needed some leverage with Winnie. I knew she was looking into buying the theatre out from under me. But then an even better idea came to mind. The chocolates."

I frowned. "So, they were meant for Winnie in the first place?"

Carter shrugged. "If Winnie *or* Julian died, it didn't really matter to me." His face darkened. "I realized my mistake after I fired her. If she wasn't there every day, I couldn't keep track of what she was planning, so I planted the painting in her house to listen to her."

The paranoia in his voice still rang through him. I remembered that feeling, but it appeared that even with the ghosts cleaning up the energy they were putting into the theatre, Carter was too far gone to be brought back by the changes they'd made.

"And Francine?" Winnie asked, her voice gaining strength.

Sighing dramatically, Carter said, "She was asking too many questions. I figured she wouldn't miss one measly box of chocolates, but she wouldn't let it go. I was worried that if you told her about the poisoned chocolates at your apartment building, she might put it together. So, she had to go. Making sure I could fire Winnie at the same time, however, proved to be the difficult part. The first time I lured Francine to the stage with a random errand, she moved out of the way too quickly. The second time, she was in the wrong spot."

An evil smile curled his lips. "The third time, I put the tape right where I wanted her, and made sure she'd be there for a while."

The duct tape. I'd seen that happen during that first rehearsal I'd watched. It had all been part of his plan. My stomach clenched with a wave of nausea.

Eyes flicking between Carter, Winnie, and the ghosts, I felt that they were reaching the end of the song. Winnie's expression was now aflame with courage. I swore she mouthed the words, "I am strong." I met her eyes and nodded, giving her the signal.

"Now!" I yelled, lunging forward onto the catwalk.

Winnie lifted her leg and brought her heel down on Carter's foot.

"Argh!" he cried. His hand released her neck.

With her newfound freedom, Winnie whipped her head back, smashing the back of her skull into Carter's nose. He pushed her forward, into my waiting arms, stumbling backward as he clutched at his face.

"Run," I whispered to Winnie.

But before we could move, a scream roared out of Carter as he lost his balance and fell from the catwalk. Winnie and I froze as we watched him tumble to the stage. A sickening crack rang out as he hit the surface. Winnie and I hugged each other tight as we stared at Carter's now limp body.

"Oh gross," Janet said, rushing away and clutching her stomach.

Nathanial and Katherine, however, peered closer.

"Rather bad luck on his part, landing on his neck like that." Katherine's cool demeanor had returned.

Winnie and I moved off the catwalk and back down to the first floor. She used her phone to call the police as I plucked mine from the stage, careful to stay clear of Carter's body. Keeping my flashlight on so I could see the ghosts, I let out an extended breath and met Ripley's eyes as she waited with the others.

"Nicely done," I whispered to them, shooting a backward glance at Winnie to ensure she was still occupied with talking to the dispatcher.

Katherine, Janet, and Nathanial beamed.

"Glad to see something good came from that production of *Newsies* after all," Ripley said. "Katherine, you have a beautiful voice."

Katherine stood straighter. "Thank you."

"Really? I thought she sounded a little pitchy. Janet was really the one who kept us all together."

Janet beamed, weaponizing the look as she directed it at Katherine. They were slipping back into their bad habits.

Ripley stepped forward. "It doesn't matter because you were all wonderful today," she said a bit forcefully.

The ghosts flinched at her tone, and nodded, reading her nonverbal cue all too clearly.

"We were," they said, glancing at one another with big smiles.

Twenty-Five

Winnie and I moved on shaky legs into the lobby, slumping onto the stairs leading up to the balcony. First of all, we needed to get away from the crumpled body of Carter. Second of all, the police would need someone to let them in when they arrived.

And boy, did they.

Being Thanksgiving, I'd expected one or two tired officers to answer the call. But officers and crime scene techs crowded the space minutes later. And they kept coming. Each time the doors opened, I checked, hoping to see Detective Anthony striding into the theatre. She'd yet to show up.

A gust of chilly air whirled around me, signaling the door having been opened once more. I looked up, seeing, not the detective, but...

"Laurie?" I stood, checking my phone quickly to make sure I hadn't missed a text or a call from him.

I'd called him about twenty minutes earlier to let him

know that I wouldn't be able to come to Thanksgiving dinner at his parents' house. The explanation I'd given him had been concise and without dramatics—a direct contrast to the way Winnie was telling it to the officer taking her statement to my left—and we'd ended the conversation planning to meet up later, once we were both back at the Morrisey.

Before saying anything, Laurie pulled me into a tight hug. The feel of him wrapped around me was something I hadn't known I'd needed. It was in that moment that I realized I'd been feeling a bit shaky, a bit ungrounded. But now that I was encompassed in Laurie's arms, in his scent, my cheek smooshed against the soft fabric of his sweater, I officially felt better.

Apparently, watching someone fall to their death from a catwalk, even a murderer, can make a girl rather unsettled.

I blinked up at him. "You left Thanksgiving?"

His brown eyes softened as they took me in. "After we got off the phone, I told my parents what had happened, and they agreed that it was more important for me to be here with the person I lo—" He stopped himself, running his teeth across his lips. "With you," he amended, proving he hadn't meant to say the first part.

Love? Even though he'd stopped himself, that was what he'd been about to say. The word sang through me. It felt right. Had we been official for less than a week? Sure. But had I been in love with the guy since I was six? Also, yes.

Given that he'd obviously stopped himself from saying the word, I decided not to push him on it and focused on a different aspect of what he'd said.

"Wait. You told them about us?" I asked. "I thought we were going to tell them together," I said, my mouth curling up at one end.

Laurie let out a rough chuckle. "Sorry. I told them within five minutes of being there today. They knew something was up; I think I was grinning like a fool." He pulled me close and whispered into my hair, "They're ecstatic, by the way."

Now I was the one grinning like a fool.

"And they say that they'd love to see you, on a day when you don't have murderers to catch," Laurie added, pulling back. He stood next to me, wrapping his arm around me as he surveyed the scene through the open doors leading toward the stage.

Discomfort lodged itself in my throat. "Well, *catch* might not be the correct word."

Laurie cocked an eyebrow. During our brief phone call, I'd only told him that it had been Carter, that he'd grabbed Winnie on our way past the theatre, and that we were both safe. I feebly gestured to the black bag, completely zipped up, that the paramedics were standing around on the stage.

"You?" Laurie breathed out the question.

I let my head wobble back and forth in what I hoped looked like a no. "Winnie. He had her up on the catwalk by the time I found them. He was going to—" My voice broke, forcing me to take a break as Laurie rubbed my back. "He was planning to push her off—both of us."

"The river of slime affected him the most out of everyone," Laurie whispered in terrified awe.

I nodded, sadness filling my heart. So much of what

Carter had done might've gone differently if he hadn't been fueled by devious, paranoid thoughts.

Needing to move past the sadness, to the good, I kept going with my story. "But the ghosts helped by sending positive, courageous vibes toward Winnie," I explained. "She stomped on his foot, broke his nose, and got away. Carter ... well, he was off-balance from Winnie's attack, and he ended up being the one who *fell*." The word was small.

Laurie's hands were on my shoulders a moment later, and he leaned down to meet my eyes. "Hey, you can't control that. He killed Francine, tried to kill Winnie, and who knows about Julian. You and Winnie did what you had to."

"Right. I'm just going to have to repeat that to myself every few minutes for a while, I think." I let out a dry laugh.

"I can help you. I'll repeat it as many times as you need." Laurie kissed the top of my head.

Just as he did so, Detective Anthony rushed into the theatre. Her gaze settled on the two of us after she took in the rest of the scene. Walking over, she lifted her chin in greeting.

"Meg, do you mind if I ask you a few questions?" The detective pulled out a notebook and glanced between me and Laurie.

"Sure." I stepped toward her, immediately missing the feel of Laurie's body next to mine, but he would be there when I was done.

As if to drive that point home, Laurie jerked his thumb over to the left, and said, "I'll go check on Winnie while the two of you talk."

The detective cleared her throat twice, seeming slightly

flustered. "I didn't know the two of you were..." She didn't finish the statement.

Her agitated state made sense. She was a detective who'd missed clues, and she didn't like to get things wrong.

"It's new," I assured her, checking on him with a quick glance.

There was something like an apology in her eyes when I looked back. It seemed like she was reliving all the times she'd been a little flirty with him in front of me before, and she was saying she was sorry for that—without speaking, of course. I nodded almost imperceptibly, letting her know there were no hard feelings.

As quickly as it showed up, the "apology" was gone. If I knew her, she'd filed away her findings, compartmentalizing any feelings she might've had, and was ready to move on.

"Okay, well, do you want to tell me what happened today?" She poised her pen over the notebook.

I explained everything. Well. Not *everything*, obviously. In my retelling, I left out the part about our ghostly help. There was a moment, however, when I wondered if it wouldn't just be easier to tell her the truth. Laurie had taken it so well. Visions of me assisting the Seattle Police Department in some kind of paranormal investigative unit flashed through my mind.

It would make for an awesome television series. A killer soundtrack of all the best grunge music played in the background as Detective Anthony and I rushed through the streets of Seattle. She'd interrogate a living suspect, and then it would cut to me talking to a ghostly informant. At the end of the credits, Ripley and I would stand back to back, and Detective Anthony would be next to us, picking a nonexistent piece of lint from her suit.

"Meg." The detective snapped in my face, annoyance creasing her forehead. "I asked if there's anything else you need to tell me."

"Oh. Uh…" I blinked, glancing once more toward Laurie. "No. That's it," I said. I had one person to share my secret with, and that was all I needed.

When I was done talking to the detective, I joined Laurie next to the ticket booth, wrapping my arm around his waist as I sank into him. He held me up.

"Are the ghosts still around?" he whispered, checking around us.

I smiled in confirmation. "They've been standing next to you for the last few minutes, actually."

He laughed nervously. "That's not disconcerting at all."

"You get used to it." I elbowed him, playfully.

Laurie looked to his left and said, "Nice to meet you three. I'm Laurie."

The ghosts, standing in front of him now, chuckled and said it was nice to meet him as well.

"Will they move on now?" Laurie asked, adding, "Now that they've helped right some of the bad energy they created here? No offense." He grimaced, again in the wrong direction.

"None taken," Katherine spoke for the group. "We deserve that."

"And more," Janet said, earning her a prickly look from Katherine.

I expected Katherine to make an offhanded comment about how Janet just *had* to add in that quip, but the spirit simply raised her chin as if she was above such pettiness and said, "As for moving on, I don't think so. I'm guessing we have *a lot* more work to do to make up for the damage we've caused."

Nathanial ran a hand down his face as if he were tired just thinking about it.

"Not yet," I told Laurie. "They're going to work on making a bigger positive impact here, once they figure out what's happening with this show, I guess. They'll need a new director."

Nathanial held up a finger, stepping forward. "They should look into Damien, actually."

"Damien?" Ripley asked. "The guy who grunts more than he speaks?"

Janet crossed her arms in defense, pouting slightly. "He was mostly like that because he hated Carter and didn't like how he bossed everyone around, but he's had dreams of being a director for ages."

"He *does* know everything there is to know about this show," Ripley said, thinking about the idea.

I filled in Laurie and he said it sounded good to him. Anyone who wasn't trying to murder people would be a vast improvement. We left, letting them plan Damien's career change as we walked home. Winnie wanted to stay, having found a new audience in Detective Anthony, and she was recounting her much more dramatic rendition of our harrowing tale.

Ripley said she'd meet me back at the apartment, leaving me and Laurie to walk home alone.

"So," I said as we made our way down the darkened city streets, practically deserted since most people were having dinner with their loved ones. "You told your parents that you love me." I pressed my lips together and glanced sidelong in his direction as we walked.

I'd decided not to let his little slip earlier go, but mostly because it made me realize that I wanted to tell him something too.

Scratching at the back of his neck, Laurie squinted one eye. "I did. It's way too soon, isn't it? I should've waited. It's definitely too soon."

"Actually..." I dragged out the word and beamed up at him. "It's perfect because I was kinda thinking that I love you too."

Laurie puffed out his cheeks in an explosive exhale. "Oh, good." Once his relief ebbed, he pulled me to a stop. "You do?"

There was that smile again.

"Yep." I leaned up to kiss him.

He laughed into the kiss. "This is officially the fastest I think I've ever said that."

"We get a special pass." I shrugged. "We've been working toward this for years."

"True." He turned serious. "I still have to pinch myself every so often to prove it's all real."

"Same." I threaded my fingers through his, and we continued walking.

Laurie cleared his throat. "My parents still have Leo since

I left their place in such a rush. My apartment will be completely empty."

I laughed. "Ripley will leave anytime we need privacy," I assured him.

"Sure, but this way we don't have to ask."

Wrapping my arm around him, I said, "Sounds perfect."

Twenty-Six

I thought having to say goodbye to Laurie a few days later would be awful. It was difficult, don't get me wrong, but I was too busy to wallow.

Between going to see Laurie's parents for the first time in years, Zoe returning from her family trip, gearing up for opening night of the musical, and visiting Julian once he woke up from his coma a week after Thanksgiving, I barely had a moment to breathe.

It was a good kind of busy, though. That Friday evening, after we got back from visiting the very contrite Julian—who promised to pay everyone back for the things he'd stolen—Ripley and I sat on the couch, chatting as we waited for Zoe. It was opening night of *Singing in the Rain,* and she'd insisted on being my date tonight since Laurie couldn't make it.

After going through every emotion possible about the show, the theatre, and the cast, I'd decided to finish my work on the sets. Beyond that, I hadn't been sure if I'd want to see the play once it opened. But during the past week, I'd finally, officially, met Petra, seen Damien come out of his shell to be a rather good—if not a little broody—director, and watched as everyone began to work together instead of fighting with one another.

The theatre had changed, already. There were still small arguments, and the normal amount of competition between fellow actors, but the hatred, paranoia, and sabotage were long gone.

Petra had decided to keep the theatre for a little while longer, but she was actively working with Winnie to figure out a co-ownership plan. Her hope was to be able to slowly step back and let Winnie take over whenever she was financially ready. Winnie had apologized for the blackmail incident, and Petra had forgiven her, as well as thanking Winnie.

Winnie had been right when she'd guessed Petra hadn't known about Damien's arrest. When she'd confronted him about it, he apologized for lying. He thought he wouldn't need to tell her since the guy dropped the charges. Yasmine had told her that Damien had kept it from her because he didn't want to get kicked out of his apartment, prompting Petra to remember the one stipulation she'd set for Damien when he'd moved in as a teenager: *you can stay with us as long as you don't get in any more trouble with the law*. Embarrassed that he still thought that was the case, even now as an adult, Petra had apologized for making him doubt that he could be honest with her.

Even Yasmine seemed to be moving on. She'd announced that *Singing in the Rain* would be her final show at the Third Avenue. She'd already gotten a part in a play at the Fifth Avenue after this show closed. She didn't think it was fair to be the owner's daughter and to be dating the director.

While the cast had gasped at her first piece of news, they'd practically fallen over with joy at her second divulgence. Apparently, she and Damien had been a couple for almost a year, feeling the need to hide it even from her mother, another thing Petra had apologized for. She said she'd been so focused on getting that position on the board, that she'd lost sight of what was truly important.

I could see a way forward for the small, historical theatre, one without alleged curses or me. I'd turned down Petra's offer to paint for their props department full time. It had been a good side project for a while, but I was ready for my next art adventure.

"Looks like everything's back to normal," Ripley said with a sigh as we decompressed from the day.

Glancing over at my best friend, I shook my head. "Nothing's ever going to be normal again."

Ripley frowned but gave me space to explain.

"Someone knows my secret now." I smiled despite myself. "I can't go back to how it used to be."

"That's good, right?" Ripley asked warily.

"Very good, but very weird. I've gone twenty-four years without letting anyone else in on it. Not even Penny knew before, and in the span of two days, I told Laurie and contemplated telling Detective Anthony as well."

Ripley huffed out a laugh. "I *did* warn you that once you tell one person, it's going to seem a lot easier to tell others. But remember, no one else is Laurie. He handled that like a champ. Better than a champ, actually. He handled that like—"

"Like Laurie," I interrupted with a grin.

"Yeah." Ripley smiled. "But he's exceptional. I don't know that you need to go around telling law enforcement or even people here at the Morrisey." Her worried gaze made my stomach drop.

"Are you leaving me?"

Ripley's eyes shuttered wider. "No. Why would you say that?"

"I don't know." I pouted. "You're giving me a bunch of advice as if you're not going to be around to tell me any of this, and you've been sneaking around a fair amount."

At that, Ripley let her shoulders slump forward. "I know. I'm sorry. I haven't been ready to talk about it."

I understood, and I hated myself a little for pushing now. "Sorry. I'll be here when you're ready."

Her brown eyes met mine. "I think I'm ready now."

My stomach clenched in anticipation. "Is it about you moving on? About why you're still here?" I wasn't sure I was ready for this conversation.

"Yeah." The word was quiet. Hollow.

My heart ached for her. "Have you found anything?"

She pressed her lips together, tight, then shook her head. "Not for lack of trying. I've been researching a lot about my foster family, trying to figure out if anything to do with them could be why I'm still around. It brought up a lot of memories, and it's why hearing about Damien being in foster care hit me so hard that day. I've never let myself dwell on them or how much I miss them. It was easier. But now..." She swallowed, unable to finish. "Anyway, I didn't find anything from that part of my life."

"Rip, I'm sorry. Is there anything I can do?" I sat forward. "We could ask Iris to help us search."

Pain flickered behind her eyes for a moment. Her lips parted, but it took her a moment before she said, "I do have an idea, but you're not going to like it."

"I'd do anything for you, Ripley. Name it. I'll help."

"I did find one clue that seems promising, but ... it's about your father."

The apartment spun around me as my skin seemed to go hot and cold all at the same time.

"What?" I reached out for the couch to steady myself. "But ... Aunt Penny said my mom didn't want me to have anything to do with him."

"Right, but doesn't that seem mysterious? The only mystery surrounding us and that night is your father. I have to check."

Swallowing, I took a beat before I answered. "Okay. I can help you look into this."

Ripley's face softened, and she whispered, "Thank you." She opened her mouth to say something else, but someone pushed the buzzer at my door.

"That must be Zoe." I smiled weakly, standing. "We should get going if we want to make the play."

"You go without me." Ripley winked. "I think I've seen it enough over the last two weeks. I'll hold down the apartment." She patted the couch cushions around her, even though her hands just went right through.

"Okay, if you're sure." I observed my best friend for a

moment waiting for her to nod that she was. Once she had, I jogged over to greet Zoe.

"Ready?" Zoe asked, pulling on a pair of gloves for the walk over.

Grabbing my jacket from the hook next to the door, and stuffing my own gloves in my pockets, I nodded. "Ready."

As I pulled the door closed behind me, I watched as Anise curled into a ball on Ripley. And I knew at that moment, scary as it was going against my mother, and my aunt's will, I would do whatever it took to make Ripley happy, to help her find peace. I locked the door behind me and hooked my arm through Zoe's.

"You're going to have to point out this hot director guy who merely grunts instead of speaking. He sounds like my perfect match." Zoe beamed.

I laughed. "I will, but I'm sorry to report that he's in love with someone else. I'm sure we can find you another broody, monosyllabic guy."

"Hmm, or maybe I should go for one who can tap-dance." She started singing the theme song to the musical we were about to see as we stepped out into the misty Seattle rain.

The Morrisey will return ...

Book four, A CRIME IN 5C, will be coming this fall. It will be full of more adventures between Meg, Ripley, Laurie, and the rest of the Morrisey gang.

The Morrisey will return ...

Meg Dawson's world is turned upside down when her Aunt Penny makes a surprise appearance at the Seattle apartment building she once called home. But beneath Penny's visit lies a mystery that could rock the very foundations of the Morrisey community.

As Penny breathes new life into the beloved Morrisey Masterpiece Classic, an annual building scavenger hunt, tensions soar and rivalries ignite among the residents. But what starts as a friendly competition soon takes a dark turn when apartment 5C is ransacked. Suddenly, the scavenger hunt transforms into a deadly game of cat and mouse, with Meg and her neighbors unwittingly caught in the crosshairs. As the stakes rise and suspicions mount, they must band together to uncover the truth before it's too late. Only one question remains: Who will emerge unscathed from this twisted tale of intrigue and betrayal.

Get your copy today!

Join Eryn's mailing list to be notified about updates.

For now, here's an illustration of Laurie and Meg by the talented Mary Livas.

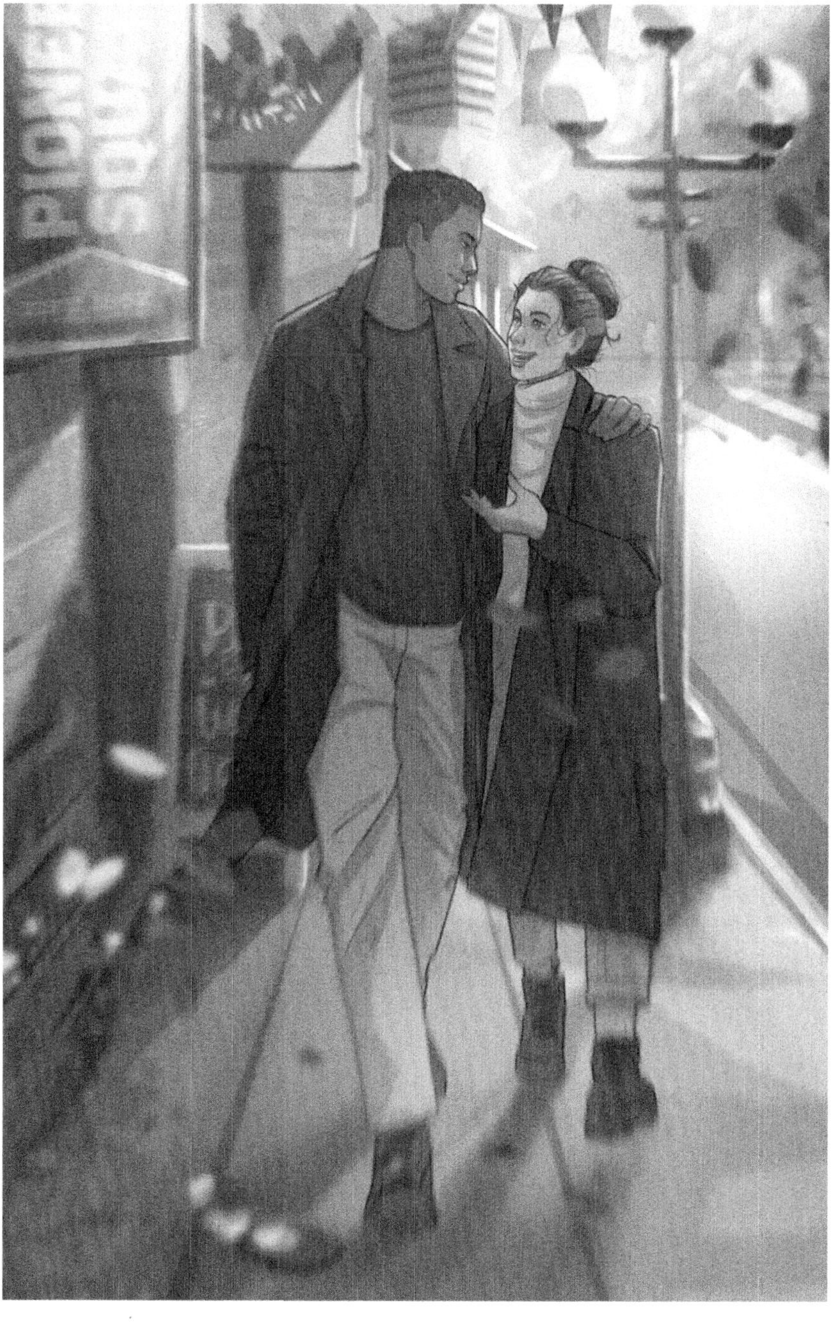

Also by Eryn Scott

STONEYBROOK MYSTERIES

Ongoing series * Farmers market * Recipes * Crime solving twins * Cats!

A Murder at the Morrisey Mystery Series

Ongoing series * Friendly ghosts * Quirky downtown Seattle building

Pebble Cove Teahouse Mysteries

Completed series * Friendly ghosts * Oregon Coast * Cat mayors

Whiskers and Words Mysteries

Ongoing series * Best friends * Bookshop full of cats

PEPPER BROOKS COZY MYSTERY SERIES

Completed series * Literary mysteries * Sweet romance * Cute dog

About the Author

Eryn Scott lives in the Pacific Northwest with her husband and their quirky animals. She loves classic literature, musicals, knitting, and hiking. She writes cozy mysteries and women's fiction.

Join her mailing list to learn about new releases and sales!

www.erynscott.com